Death of a Clown
Catherine McCarthy

Sobelo Books

Copyright © 2025 by Catherine McCarthy

All rights reserved.

No part of this publication may be reproduced, distributed, or transmitted in any form or by any means, including photocopying, recording, or other electronic or mechanical methods, without the prior written permission of the publisher, except as permitted by U.S. copyright law. For permission requests, contact lucas@sobelo books.com.

The story, all names, characters, and incidents portrayed in this production are fictitious. No identification with actual persons (living or deceased), places, buildings, and products is intended or should be inferred.

Book Cover by Tony Evans

Formatted and published by Sobelo Books

ISBN (paperback): 978-1-965389-09-6
ISBN (ebook): 978-1-965389-08-9

First edition, 2025

Also by Catherine McCarthy

The House at the End of Lacelean Street
The Wolf and the Favour
Mosaic
A Moonlit Path of Madness
Immortelle
Mists and Megaliths
Door and other twisted tales

Contents

Dedication

This story is dedicated to all those who, at some point or other, find themselves lost on the path of life.
Be brave! Be bold! And remember, you only get one shot at this glorious shit show.

1

Suspended upside down on a rope ladder, fifteen feet above the audience, Chester Brown experiences a lightbulb moment of utter despair. At this moment, the enraptured crowd appear demented. It is not he who holds them captive but they him. Snarling teeth and shadowed eyes, they wear their brows as villainous moustaches, a hundred Genghis Khan and his evil offspring. Chester's heart is a pounding war drum, his chalk-white face a mask of deceit, for the skin beneath it is marshmallow pale and clammy.

Arms folded in feigned nonchalance, he whistles a tune, which is all part of the act, for in truth he feels far from jolly. An umbilical cord between this life and the life he desires has been severed by an invisible hand, so much so that he pictures himself falling...falling...falling through the air until he lands on the ground, never to wake. A moment of lucidity elbows its way in. Why now? Couldn't there have been a more suitable moment to be dealt an epiphany?

Turning his gaze away from the crowd, he faces the ceiling. A flock of illusory terns flap and screech all around him, and when he plucks a potato chip from his breast pocket and feeds it to a swooping gull the audience roars with laughter. This he hears rather than sees because each and every face is a morphed smudge of charcoal, blurred around the edges. Coloured lights sweep across their faces, turning grey flesh purple, orange, green, each image as grotesque as the next.

By some miracle, the muscles around Chester's core do as he bids them and pull him upright. He sets the ladder in motion, his left hand held waving and left foot dangling free. A surge of fear shoots along his spine, but it is not because he fears falling. What Chester fears is the thought that he will have to repeat the same act tomorrow...and the next day...and the next, like some kind of automaton, all in the name of entertainment.

The swinging ladder slows and Chester dismounts, tumbling in an exaggerated manner and blowing the audience a kiss before dashing off-stage. Three steps from the tunnel exit, he trips and falls. Part of the performance, the audience believes, so they roar louder and clap harder. Little do they know his spine has turned to rubble; his limbs to sand. He makes it as far as the dressing-room before collapsing in a heap on the floor.

It takes several minutes before his heart slows to an acceptable pace. Using the basin as a prop, he pulls himself to his feet, gulps cold water from the tap, then studies his reflection in the mirror. What just happened out there? The roar of the crowd vibrates in his ears even now, an auditory hallucination, but nonetheless terrifying. The crystal teardrop attached to the outer corner of his eye winks; the stark white greasepaint around his mouth shines slick with saliva and sweat.

He closes the toilet seat and slumps down, head in hands. For almost two decades he has performed his duties as a clown, and not once has he experienced such anxiety, not even when the legendary Oleg Poletsky came to watch his troupe perform. Inhaling deep and long through his nose, he attempts to stem the well of fear that rises to his throat.

This is not about the audience; this is about Chester's very existence. Eyes closed tight, he focusses on his breathing. He knows without a shadow of doubt that he cannot—will not—perform any longer. His belief in the life he has lived until now is a snuffed candle. The Clown God, Cholly, a figment of the imagination, a legendary figure created to make Chester and the rest of his kin accept the life that has been chosen for them.

Cholly does not exist.

Chester Brown, the tragic clown, no longer exists.

Removing his make-up in front of the mirror for what he is determined will be the last time feels like an act of purification. Each layer of grease paint he removes, each sparkle of glitter he extinguishes reveals more and more of his true self. He examines his reflection: naked skin, raw from scrubbing. Forehead lines deeper than they should be for a twenty-nine-year-old. Kind eyes, nutmeg brown but shadowed underneath, as if years of painting on black teardrops has stained the skin indelibly. Tonight, he will not leave a single smudge behind.

The sense of relief turns to dismay as he studies his nose. No matter how much grease paint he removes, the incriminating feature will always be there. The bulbous nose. He has worn the mark of the clown since birth, as have his siblings, but whereas they rejoice in it, he detests it. He stares down at his feet, another give-away. Size twenty. Each pair of shoes he buys from The Clown Emporium are wearable barges.

"When I was carrying you, there were times when I thought you'd crack a rib," his mother has joked on many occasions.

He had found the anecdote amusing as a child, but not now. Now it reminds him that no matter what, he will bear the curse of his clown characteristics forever, at least in the physical sense.

Chester strips and hangs up his suit, promising never to wear it again. Crumpled off-white shirt, checked trousers that sit well above the waist, black braces the only thing that stops them falling down. A fool's garments. They sag on the peg, deflated. Any trace of the man who has worn the same outfit day in, day out, year in, year out has dissipated into thin air. Finally, he removes the shiny black boots, eighteen inches long, a bright purple lace on the left, a bright orange lace on the right. How ridiculous they make him look.

He wiggles his toes, blanching at the hideous length of them. Would it be possible for a surgeon to reduce the size of his feet? And what about his nose? He pinches the flesh either side of the cartilage. He has read that rhinoplasty works miracles for some people. He covers his nose with a hand, considering how such an operation might alter his features. And yet deep down he knows he is deceiving himself. Even if such changes were possible, they would only be skin deep. It is his mind that would need to make the biggest adjustment.

How long has he felt this way? Did he really experience an epiphany out there tonight, or have the feelings of disassociation been budding for a while? Gathering dust in the corner like a worn-out piece of furniture. Truth be told, it is the latter. In fact, he has never felt he belonged, not really.

Heartsore and weary, Chester changes into a white shirt and black, baggy trousers that distract from the size of his feet. A wide-brimmed hat attempts to hide his bulbous nose.

"Chester," he says to the mirror. His voice is pitched high, a poor imitation of his mother's. "I know you find it amusing, but please don't let Father Roly catch you wearing that hat. You know how he is. He would consider such an accessory blasphemous."

He shakes his head and frowns. Those are not his mother's words. His mother is incapable of formulating such a sentence. He tries again, his vocabulary more accurate this time, his accent thicker, coarser. "For Cholly's sake, Chester, don't let Father Roly catch you in that hat. He'll have you in the confessional before you can say Bobo's your uncle! Be proud of who you are!"

A smile plays at the corners of his mouth, though fails to make it as far as his eyes. He loves his mother. In fact, he loves all of his family, but they do not understand him. They never have.

His stomach flips at the thought of telling them what he intends to do. And yet it must be done.

A knock on the dressing-room door startles him. He is not in the mood for idle conversation, so he ignores it.

"Chester? You in there?"

It is the rumbling voice of Duke Hellington, ringmaster and theatre manager. Chester holds his breath and prays he locked the door behind him. If he were to speak to Duke right now, he is certain he would be unable to hide his feelings. They would be written all over his face. Disenchantment, despair, desperation.

In all likelihood, he would blurt out his intentions to leave the troupe and never return.

"Chester?" Once more, then with a huff he hears the master leave. Had Duke been watching Chester's performance tonight? Had he sensed something amiss? And why on earth does Chester feel so guilty? The answer to the last question lies deep within his heart, tucked inside the left ventricle if the stab of pain is anything to go by. Indoctrination, and yet the rest of them do not see it. Either that, or they accept it without challenge because it is easier to do so, it requires less effort and Cholly forbid, far less thought.

Selfish. Ungrateful. Ideas above his station. That is what they would say if they knew how he felt. Brought up to believe that graduating from Clown School and entering the world of theatre and circus is an honour, he has known no other life. How many times has he been reminded that those who failed to make the grade were subjected to a life of servitude, working either in the service industries to provide for the needs of the *clown elite*, or worse still jobless and left to fend for themselves.

Only ten percent of you will make the grade and be offered a position in the theatre. The headmaster's voice is clear in his head, though he graduated almost two decades ago. Has it really done him a favour though?

Chester swallows hard, the muscles in his throat doing their damnedest to choke him. Sweat beads on his forehead, trickles down his spine. Yet his extremities tingle with cold. Before panic consumes him entirely, he grabs his overcoat and keys and sneaks out the back exit.

A chill wind hits him full in the face, feasting on skin red raw from rubbing. Chester hoists his coat collar and hurries along the street, head bowed, eyes on the pavement, as is his way.

After a hundred yards or so he passes by the brightly painted church, the place where they congregate on Monday evenings, their *Sabbath*, in praise of The Great Clown god, Cholly. He does not raise his head; he cannot bear to look at the place right now.

A left turn, past the little school where young clowns are taught the tricks of the trade before being baptized into the faith at the age of ten. A swift glance in the direction of the playground is all it takes to resurrect the sense of dread. Despite the encroaching darkness, it is possible to make out the row of rainbow coloured air walkers, the balance beams and hurdles that increase in size and difficulty.

As a clownet, Chester had mastered the dexterous skills with ease, his natural physique perfectly suited to physical stunts and ludicrous antics. It was the slapstick humour he found more difficult. Chester was not, by nature, funny, which was why they baptized him into the Sacred Order of Tragicomedy and from that day forward expected him to spend the rest of his life performing the role of a wisecracking funnyman, one whose coping mechanism for his hopelessness was humour. A paradox like no other. Little did he know back then how prophetic it would be.

At the corner of the junction looms the place he calls home. An L shaped four-storey building built of red brick and dressed in yellow stone, originally built to house a range of artisan workshops, now converted to flats and bedsits.

Fumbling for his keys, he takes the stairs to the third floor two at a time, desperate to reach sanctuary.

Greeted by the soft purr of Arlo, his Abyssinian, the knot in his stomach loosens a tad. He stoops to pick the cat up before rubbing his face in his soft fur. "Hey, Arlo, how ya been?"

Arlo meets his gaze, long ears pricked and moss-green eyes, wise as Feste. He grants Chester a moment's comfort before freeing himself from his arms and leaping onto the sofa.

Unable to face the thought of food, Chester heats a pot of coffee, then settles at his desk. His fingers fumble beneath the wood until he hears a click. He slides the notebook from its hiding place, selects his favourite fountain pen from the stand and a bottle of dark blue ink, and begins to write.

The Raven and the Tightrope Walker
by Runo Quill

The nom de plume he had chosen at the age of eight stands proud against the creamy-white paper; the curve of each letter softens his mood.

For the next few hours, Chester the Clown will cease to exist.

The Raven and the Tightrope Walker

by Runo Quill

The boy named Zar stopped in his tracks and pointed towards the heavens. "Look, Mother. There's a man walking across the sky!"

His mother did not raise her head. Instead, she slapped his hand and told him not to stare at the sun.

Zar's toes tap-danced on the cobbles. "But he's walking across the sky. You must look." Shielding his eyes, he squinted upwards, mouth agape and eyes bright as stars.

Zar was granted but a few seconds of entertainment before his mother whisked him down the road by his elbow.

"What have I always told you?" she said, mouth pinched and brows furrowed. "We must never look up, only where we're heading." She tutted, and each click of her tongue felt like a curse. "There's nothing up there for the likes of us. The sky is for dreamers."

As if to prove her wrong, a raven swooped low, issuing a throaty chortle of mirth.

Zar tugged and twisted from her grasp, desperate to see where the man who walked the sky would go next, but his mother's grip was a vice.

Ten years passed by, and Zar stood on the brink of manhood. He had never forgotten the man who walked across the sky. The image of the black-clad hero was indelibly printed on his retinas.

The road ahead was paved with repetition, and Zar had no intention of following it. One night, before the sun stole a glimpse of the world, he packed a knapsack and headed away from the village.

As he crept down the road, a raven took flight from an old yew tree and came to land on his shoulder. Other than the flap of its wings it made no sound because it did not want to betray its new friend.

Zar met the raven eye to eye and knew in his heart it was the same bird that had mocked his mother all those years ago.

Zar and the raven headed into the woods. Thick and dense with beech and ash it concealed him from the prying eyes of those who would wish to thwart his adventure.

From out the knapsack he fetched a coil of rope as thick as a serpent and twice as strong and secured it three feet above the ground to the tree trunks. He searched the woods until he found the straightest branch he could to help him balance—a sycamore, six feet long and dry as cinder.

Time and time again Zar toppled from the rope but refused to give up. At the core of his being, cradled between navel and backbone, sat his centre of gravity, and Zar knew that in order to master the tightrope the two needed to become the best of friends.

Many bumps and bruises later, Zar found himself able to cross the void from ash to beech without falling.

"Kraa!" said the raven, hopping onto his shoulder and nipping his ear with its long beak. "Kraa! Kraa!" which Zar knew meant: *See, I knew you could do it. Aim high, and never allow the apathy of others to shatter your dreams.*

Zar and the raven headed deeper into the woods where they made a bed of sweet-smelling spruce and watched as the sun set the sky on fire.

Late into the night Zar told the raven tales of sorrow and strife, and in exchange, the raven spoke of long forgotten secrets from the spirit world.

Months became years, and years became decades, and Zar and the raven travelled the world as friends do. Together they crossed the mountains of Switzerland, the Château de Chantilly, the peaks of Yosemite, and even the falls of Niagara. The raven on the wing, and Zar on the tightrope, but never too far apart.

Great crowds gathered to see them, and Zar and the raven grew famous.

One night, having crossed the Taimu mountain of China, Zar suddenly declared he wished to return home.

The raven took to the wing, turning somersaults in the air and shrieking in protest, but Zar would not be deterred. It sang a song of premonition, mimicking the words Zar had spoken when first they'd met. "*Sky!*" it croaked, in a perfect parody of Zar's own voice. "*Sky,*" and "*Frreee!*" but Zar folded his arms, shook his head, and refused to be dissuaded.

"I want to go home," he said, stroking the storm-clouds and summer skies that were the raven's feathers. "I wish to see my people one last time. Perhaps their outlook has changed."

The raven nestled its head in Zar's chest, and a single tear of dew trickled down its beak, for he knew the unlikelihood of such a thing.

A smog skulked over the village square as Zar entered, concealing him from view. The smell of woodsmoke and tannin tainted his tongue as he made his way towards the inn that was the hub of the village.

The raven perched on his shoulder, sharp talons biting the flesh as it hopped from one toe to another.

A thick silence fell as Zar opened the inn door and stepped inside. All eyes turned to look at the stranger who had dared to enter their domain.

"No birds allowed," the landlord barked in the voice of a jackal. He shook a filthy cloth, as if to shoo them outside.

Zar stood his ground. "Has anyone seen my mother?" he said without so much as a quiver. The raven ruffled its tail feather and stuck out its chest as it eyed the crowd.

The landlord's mouth fell open; his eyes searched Zar's face for signs of belonging but found none. For Zar had been gone too long and had lost the grimace and gripe of the rest of them.

"It's Mega's son," a voice at the back piped up. "I remember the cut of his jib."

Mega was summoned to the inn, but instead of shedding tears of joy she shrieked with the anger of one jilted. "Where have you been all these years?" she said, shaking a fist at her son. "And who do you think you are, coming in here with that demon on your shoulder and a glint in your eye?"

Zar swallowed the lump that formed in his throat. "Where have I been? Oh, Mother, the sights I have seen. Do you remember how you scolded me for looking towards the sky?"

She puckered her lips and narrowed her eyes but said not a word.

"I tell you, Mother, until you have seen the world from a great height you have not lived."

She tapped her foot and folded her arms, unconvinced. "Do you mock me?" she said. She waved an arm at those gathered who were enjoying the spectacle with grinning teeth and nodding heads. "Do you belittle us with your fancy ways? You never did belong here." And with that, she turned on her heels and stomped from the inn, slamming the door behind her.

The raven croaked and spluttered. "*Sky,*" it said, too close to Zar's ear.

So Zar stepped back to the threshold. "Meet me at the river at sundown," he said to those who had gathered.

In all of the places, in all of the world, not once had Zar felt afraid of walking the tightrope. Today, though, he was afraid. Years it had taken for him to find the courage to reach for the stars, decades even, and there were moments he felt he had touched them. High above the rooftops, the lakes, and the rivers, he felt free as a bird. But here, in the place he was born, the weight of the world pressed him into the earth until he thought he might suffocate.

"You were right," he said to the raven. "Nothing has changed. I should have listened."

The raven's head bowed low in mourning, but it did its best to hide its contempt.

"But now I am here, I must show them how much I have achieved."

With expert hands and feet, he climbed to the top of a sturdy elm and fastened the first hook, twisting and tugging to test its strength more zealously than usual. Having secured the rope, he swung with the agility of a gibbon, across to the other side of the river where he did the same to another tree. Just fifteen feet or so high, nothing compared to what he was used to, and yet it seemed an impossible height.

The raven stood on the branch of a willow that dipped its long arms into the water. Today, for the first time, it would not accompany Zar on his walk across the river. Instead, it would wait on the opposite bank, tiny black heart in its mouth and feathers atremble. If Zar made it safely across, it was certain the two of them would take their leave and travel far and away from this place of blindness. For the raven knew that despite being able to see, the people of this place had chosen to live their lives in the realm of the blind.

As the sun rose above the mountain and spread its rays across the river, crowds gathered.

Perched high above their heads, Zar watched the water tumble and gurgle, froth and spit, eager for him to make a mistake. For the river coursed through their veins, not his. Day after day, year after year, it made the same journey they did with no longing to change direction.

Sneers and smirks, gripes and groans, the crowd jostled for position until Zar called them to attention. Then, as one, they held their breath and watched as Zar stepped out of the elm's golden crown and onto the taut rope.

Not daring to look, the raven tucked its head into its chest and dug its talons deep into the willow's flesh.

Halfway across, it seemed as though Zar would make it. Frayed nerves had bonded and turned to steel, and his heart beat steady and calm. He paused for a moment, daring to glance down at the crowd. The dove grey hair of his mother caught his eye, though she had not come in peace.

"Look at me," he said without so much as a quiver. "This is how it feels to raise your sights and see the world from above." He laughed then, a small chuckle, not a hearty boom, and in doing so failed to notice his brother raise a hand and throw the blade into the air. Even if he had, he would not have recognized him, for his brother had grown fat and mealy-mouthed.

A split second was all it took for the blade to strike its target. Zar tumbled out of the sky and into the bloodthirsty mouth of the river, hitting his head on a boulder as he landed. No attempt was made to save him; instead, the crowd cheered and crowed. They clapped his brother on the shoulder before turning their backs on the river and heading for home.

The raven was distraught. It fretted and floundered, croaked and cawed, but Zar did not surface. Perched atop the boulder, the raven watched the water wash Zar's blood away, thus removing the evidence. Soon, only the rumble of the river's hunger could be heard, and the raven despaired at its greed. It hung its head low and waited, certain Zar would find a way to comfort it.

And indeed, he did. As the sun set on the horizon, and nocturnal eyes glinted among the trees, from the depths of the water the raven heard a familiar voice.

"Fetch me the rope," it said, the words a burble and babble, though nonetheless distinguishable. "Fetch me the rope, and I will avenge us."

So the raven did as Zar asked. It flew to the treetop and pecked and plucked until the rope frayed and tore, then it carried the rope in its beak and perched once more on the boulder.

A grey and wrinkled limb dashed from the surface and snatched the rope from the raven's beak, then the raven was alone once more.

The raven spent the rest of its life in the woods. Each time it heard the lap of a boat or the splash of a swimmer it would hurry to the river's edge, eager to see what might happen.

As for the ghost of the tightrope walker, it remained on the riverbed for a hundred years, casting its coiled rope and dragging each and every villager who dared to enter to a watery grave.

If you listened carefully, you might hear these words, spoken in a reedy whisper that grew fainter as the years passed by...

"Now you know how it feels to be dragged to the bottom and never allowed to rise."

A century later, when none of the villagers or their descendants remained and the village was populated with those who could see, the raven and ghost soared to a height far greater than they had ever climbed before and were never seen again.

2

Chester opens the curtains and looks down on a street dressed in a fine gauze of mizzle, one that attempts to subdue the brightly coloured shops and cafes that make up this part of Clown Quarter. Krusty's Cakes, with its familiar aroma of cinnamon and sugar, fails to whet his appetite this morning, and the lurid candy-stripes of the make-up store threatens to bring on a migraine.

Arlo purrs and weaves a figure of eight between his bare feet, unperturbed by their obscene length. Chester steps into the slippers his brother had bought him for his mirthday, to which his mother had sewn bright red pompoms despite her knowing how much he loathed his feet and nose. He hadn't the heart to throw them in the trash, especially since everyone in the family found them amusing.

"They're pompoms, not noses, you fool," she had said when he'd grimaced, and yet he knew she was having a stab at him.

This was part of the problem. Everyone in this whole jolly community felt the need to laugh at everything. Until someone dared to question their beliefs, that is. It was not so funny then.

Chester remembers occasions when he would be in a roomful of people, watching them roll around with laughter, while for him the joke missed its mark by a mile. The insincerity of their joviality felt forced, but anyone noticing his blank expression would dig him in the ribs and tell him to cheer up. He was a sad clown. So what? As far as they were concerned it did not give him the right to be miserable. But they were wrong. Miserable was not the correct term to describe how he felt. Alienated, yes. Desperate to escape even, but not miserable. Sick of the slapstick. Sick of the buffoonery. Why, he was even sick of the sight of them.

Having fed Arlo, he brews a fresh pot of coffee and skims the story he had written the previous night, flinching at his errors and scribbling bright red notes in the margin. The image of the tightrope walker balancing across a vast waterfall, his black-winged companion cheering him on, sparks an idea, a potential escape route from the monotony of his routine. If only he can get the ringmaster to agree.

Grabbing the bull by the horns, Chester shrugs into his overcoat and heads for the theatre. This morning's mizzle has dissipated into thin air, leaving in its wake a bright sky and icy temperatures.

The streets of Clown Quarter wear a feigned brightness as winter sun turns their lurid colours even bolder. Dazzled by the rays, Chester's eyes water and his nose condenses the frosty air to deliver a constant stream of snot. He digs about in his pocket for a handkerchief and blows hard.

By the time he reaches the theatre he is sweating, despite the cold. His oversized feet catch on the stone steps, and he plummets head-first into the door. He is out of sorts and therefore clumsy. Marina sits in the ticket booth, counting the previous day's takings. She eyes him suspiciously as he bursts through the door.

"You're early." Cerise lips and huge blue eyes, she wears a bright pink taffeta dress. An oversized doll in a child's clothing.

Chester sniffs. "I need to speak with Duke. Is he about?"

Marina raises a perfectly arched eyebrow. "In his office last I looked, though you might wanna wear a gum shield if you intend to ask for a raise. He's not in the best of moods."

Chester's heart plummets. He has always avoided confrontation of any kind, which is part of the reason he finds himself in his current predicament. A cursory nod, then he unhitches the red-rope barrier that separates public and staff and skulks along the narrow corridor towards the master's office.

Duke Hellington, a brass plaque reads, *Master of Ceremonies*. In all the years he has worked for him, Chester has never heard Duke referred to by his title. An etched glass panel morphs the master's figure into a grotesque shape, sharpening Chester's nerves into razorblades. He taps the door with a single knuckle and waits.

"Come in!" Brusque and impatient, like September wasps.

Chester enters and stands frozen.

"Ah, Chester." Duke motions to the chair across from his desk. "Sit down, sit down. I'm glad you've come."

Remembering the knock on his dressing-room door the previous night, Chester decides to wait for Duke to speak first. In any case, his tongue feels swollen. He is not certain the words he has come to say will form right now.

Duke slams a hand down on the file on the desk in front of him. "Grim Peeper," he says. "Our latest protege. Ten-years-old, fresh from school." He waits for Chester to say something, and when he does not, he continues. "I'd like you to mentor him. He shows great promise."

Chester is lost for words. He gapes like a fish out of water. "I—I. Actually, Duke, I came to say—" The master's frown steals the end of his sentence and leaves him floundering.

"He'll start tomorrow. I've invited him to tonight's performance and instructed him to study you closely." He opens the file on his desk and taps a black and white photograph of Chester before turning his frown into a grin. "You'll be pleased to hear you're famous. I didn't need to show him the photograph; he already knows who you are."

Chester should be pleased, and yet he is not. In fact, it makes him feel worse. A young child, one who in all likelihood considers him a hero, is about to be sorely disappointed. He scratches his head, uncertain of what to say. "Actually, Duke, I wonder if I might have a word." He runs a dry tongue around his mouth. "I've been feeling out of sorts lately and thought a change might do me good."

"A *change*?" The master's tone is ascetic. "What on earth do you mean?"

"Well I—" Flushed face, sweaty palms. "I thought perhaps I might try the tightrope."

Hands flat on the desk, the master booms. "The *tightrope*?" He laughs so loud that small items on his desk quake with fear. "The tightrope you say?" He removes his spectacles and wipes them in the sleeve of his shirt, then peers at Chester as if seeing him for the first time.

Chester does not laugh. Quite the opposite. His fists are clenched; his jaw fused. "I am perfectly serious." To his dismay, tears well behind his eyes. If they were to spill, he would run from the room and never return. He swallows hard and gathers himself. "I need a change, that's all. I've felt stifled of late. I mean, the same thing day in, day out for almost two decades. It's enough to drive a man insane."

The master's ruddy glee fades to grey. He leans back in his chair and studies Chester, searching for signs of insincerity. When he finds none, he speaks. "Chester, the tightrope? With those feet?" He smothers a grin with his hand. "Seriously, you could not have made a more ludicrous suggestion. In all honesty, I'm having difficulty believing you're not pulling my leg."

Chester's face burns. Why did he not consider the size of his feet? What on earth was he thinking? He takes a deep, stuttering breath and shakes his head. "I'm sorry," he says, "I—I don't know what to say." Head bowed low, he picks up his hat and leaves.

As he passes the ticket booth, Marina raises her head but does not need to ask how the meeting went. His ashen complexion speaks volumes.

Duke's request has thrown him into a quandary. Remembering how impressionable he was at the age of ten he is reluctant to let the young protege down, and yet the thought of dressing up in costume tonight and performing again makes him feel physically sick. What an idiot! How could he have considered the tightrope as a change of direction?

Frosty pavements sparkle as he continues along the street, reminding him that not everything that glitters is gold. Sometimes shiny things will trip you up.

Take money for example, yes one cannot exist without it, and Chester has been frugal over the years and has amassed a substantial savings pot, but it has not made him happy. In fact, the need to earn a crust is the sole reason he is still here, or at least that is what he convinces himself. Were he to refuse to do any more performances his income would cease to exist, and his savings would soon run dry. Therein lies the rub; the vicious cycle of having to endure mundanity in order to survive.

His size twenties stomp along the pavement, steering him in an unconscious direction. Chester is so consumed with the idiocy of his suggestion of a change in career that he fails to consider where he is heading. Why the tightrope? Is it because of the story he had written the previous night, or is there another reason? Perhaps the notion of a challenge did it, a challenge that would not only test his physical prowess but also his nerve. He thinks back to the previous night at the theatre, to the moment the epiphany struck. He had been elevated above the audience on a ladder and upside down. The memory sends a shiver down his spine, and yet he had performed the trick on several occasions, therefore it was not the height that initiated the panic.

Each breath he takes is a cloud of concern, mimicking his indecision, and yet he knows that despite his determination never to don the clown costume again, he is, at present, caught in a trap. He will have to perform tonight, if only for the sake of the young protege who will be coming to watch.

Head down and thoughts in turmoil, he fails to notice the colour change in his surroundings. His feet have led him away from Clown Quarter towards a far less vibrant part of the city—Magicians' Quarter.

A sense of greyness seeps into his subconscious, encouraging him to raise his head. Chester stops in his tracks and bites his lower lip in thought. Towering buildings, dark and ominous with black carriages, black horses, monochrome awnings above shops and offices. And yet he smiles. He adores this part of the city with its smart cafes and fancy restaurants, even though he has not visited for quite some time. Above all, he loves the Reading Rooms, situated on the corner of Pentacle Avenue, the place where five streets intercept. The city's only place of study is situated here because magic is the most mentally challenging of all theatre acts, or so Chester believes. His stomach churns with longing. Why did he have the misfortune to be born a clown and not a magician?

Turning down the collar of his overcoat in an attempt to look a little smarter, he peers across the road to where a lady and gent examine a menu displayed in a cafe window. His stomach rumbles. Should he grab a late breakfast? He does not need to return to the theatre until six o'clock, but the thought of sitting alone in an eatery in this part of town makes him quake. His old coat, frayed around the cuffs, the enormous shoes, and above all, his bulbous nose. He cannot do it.

A street vendor selling baked potatoes and peas catches his eye, so instead of the cafe Chester approaches the cart and makes a purchase, grateful for the fact that the vendor does not so much as raise an eyebrow at a clown who has absconded from his district. And yet he knows it is a rare occurrence. His peers rarely venture out of Clown Quarter, and if they do, they veer towards the acrobatic and trapeze artists' part of the city, those with whom they have far more in common.

Chester hugs a street corner, a lamppost acting as a prop while he eats, and observes the comings and goings from beneath the wide brim of his hat.

The Reading Rooms are situated up a flight of steps, steps that have not been designed to cater for his clown feet. He mounts them with care, eager not to make a fool of himself as he had done that morning at the theatre.

An elderly librarian peers over her spectacles as he enters, and Chester pinches his nose before addressing her. "Good morning," he says, conscious of the fact that he has strayed beyond his district.

She seems to recognize him, for she smiles widely. "Well hello there. I haven't seen you here for some time."

He gives a little cough. How can he tell her it was not his intention to come today either, but that his feet had led the way without his consent? "Is it all right if I—" He gestures towards the double doors that separate reception from reading rooms.

"Why, of course." She gives a little wink and her pale eyes glisten. There's magic in those eyes, Chester thinks. Not only because of what she must have read over the years, but because of the majesty of this place.

Stepping through the double doors is like stepping into another world. The aroma of camphor and polish, ink and paper. A woody vanilla scent. He inhales deeply before assessing the room's layout. The vast space looks a little different today. Same built-in bookcases line the room with their cloak of knowledge; same ladders for reaching the high shelves—dark oak and narrower at the top. But now, instead of one central desk dominating the centre of the room, there are at least six smaller desks, interspersed throughout. This pleases him, as he prefers to have his own space when reading.

Close by, a gentleman dressed head to toe in black and carrying a pack of playing cards in his breast pocket – the Queen of Hearts displayed to perfection – pays him a cursory glance before continuing his book search. Archaeology, Chester notes, and cannot help but wonder why a magician might want to study archaeology. But who is he to judge? A clown, here to study philosophy. He laughs out loud at how ludicrous it seems, and the magician frowns at him from beneath his top hat. If only his mother could see him now, or worse still, one of his brothers. They would baulk and call him a traitor.

He chooses a table in the far corner, where he will be partly concealed by a nautical armillary globe on a stand and removes his coat before browsing the shelves.

The philosophy section is not vast, in fact it consists of half a bookcase, but he is certain new titles have been added since his last visit. Hegel, Kant, both of whom he has read on previous occasions. He skims the shelves, determined to find something new, something that questions organized religion, Kierkegaard perhaps or Voltaire, both of whom he finds challenging.

What he finds instead makes him gasp.

A slender volume, bound in ox-blood leather, the front of which is titled: *Death of a Clown; Birth of an Artist.*

No author's name on either cover or title page. It speaks to him on such a personal level he cannot help but be intrigued. Both cover and pages appear brand new. No yellowing paper or scuffed leather; no cracked spine or stains, at least none that he can see, and yet it bears no date either. He brings it close to his nose and inhales: a vanilla-like scent that reminds him of spun sugar with a hint of autumn woods.

He takes it to the desk and skims the contents page. At first glance, it is not apparent whether the book is fiction or non-fiction. What stands out most is the fact that it is handwritten. In that case it must be a one-off.

A chapter list reads: *Chapter One, Florence*. A travel guide, perhaps, and yet the title does not suggest as much. But what about the other chapters? The list continues with: *Chapter Two, Chapter Three* etc. but does not name the destination.

Death of a Clown; Birth of an Artist. The title could have been written with Chester in mind, the synchrony is astonishing, but why has it been placed in the Philosophy section? Surely a mistake. Either that, or someone has moved it.

The magician, who is seated at the far end of the room, is focussed on his choice of reading matter. Whatever he has chosen from the Archaeology bookcase appears to be waging war on his wit, as his frown lines are deep.

Chester turns his attention back to the book. It has to be more than coincidence. He is convinced that somehow the book has been waiting for him. He opens it to the preface and begins to read...

Since as far back as I can remember, I believe from around the age of four, I felt a keen sense that something was wrong with me.

At that moment, having read the opening sentence, Chester's mind is made up. He does something he has never done before in the whole of his life—one eye on the magician, he dons his overcoat and secrets the book inside the inner pocket. An act of theft, but he knows that even if he could persuade the librarian to allow him to borrow the book, he could not bear to return it afterwards.

Chester gets to his feet and exits the reading room, bidding the librarian a tip of his hat, before hurrying down the steps and onto the streets of the monochromatic world of Magicians' Quarter.

Death of a Clown; Birth of an Artist

Preface

Since as far back as I can remember, I believe from around the age of four, I felt a keen sense that something was wrong with me. Born into an alley of clowns, all of whom were dedicated to the profession and sought no other kind of life, I struggled to keep the faith. As a clownet I kept my true feelings hidden, believing I was the one in the wrong and that should I declare my misery I would be seen as a traitor, a misfit, an apostate.

Not until I graduated at the age of ten did I begin to see my world for what it was—a farcical illusion of feigned cheer, perpetuated by those whose chief aim in life it was to maintain the status quo, and in doing so grant themselves permission not to think or to question. Of course, at such a young age I was unable to change my situation and blamed myself for being different.

As my despair deepened, I began to question the existence of the Clown God, Cholly, and saw my religion as a means to indoctrination and acceptance without question. A control mechanism, if you like.

For years I tried to adapt, wanting nothing more than to be normal and to fit the role intended for me (that of a tragic clown), but of course I failed.

I grew to detest the constant joviality, the pranks, the slapstick. More than that though, I began to despise the way I looked and the features that marked me out as a clown—the bulbous nose, gigantic feet, the creases on my forehead that seemed to deepen daily as a result of being overly expressive, and in the end it drove me to the point where I knew that if I didn't escape I would lose my mind.

Hence this journal, and hence the pilgrimage I am about to take you on. It is a journey of self-discovery, the story of a clown who managed to escape his bounds and shed his clownishness once and for all.

Oh, and by the way, since I have not introduced myself (how rude of me), I shall do so now, though instead of my birth name I will give you the name I travelled by. My name is Geppetto. Yes, that's right, I named myself after the father of a marionette, carved from an enchanted piece of wood. Why, you might ask? Because as a child I made an emotional connection to the story—Pinocchio's long nose, his feet, once charred to cinders so that his father, Geppetto, found it necessary to make him a new pair, which was more than he deserved. And then of course there is Geppetto's journey, his search for Pinocchio, quite different to my own but nonetheless poignant.

Are you ready? We begin in Florence, Italy, the place where The Story of a Puppet was written and the place I fled to first.

Chester is so enamoured by what he reads that even the thought of having to go to work does not faze him. He feeds Arlo, and himself, then settles on the sofa to read.

He knows very little about Florence, in fact, were you to ask him to tell you what he knows he would say it was once the capital of Italy and that it is famous for culture and the arts. That is the sum of his knowledge. Oh, and perhaps one more thing...he loves how the place sounds—Florence. It suggests a flourish of flowers and grand buildings.

According to the journal, his predecessor (for this is how he views the clown, Geppetto) had made Florence his first port of call having travelled by ferry from Dover to Calais, then by train into Switzerland and crossing the Alps before journeying onward by whatever means he could with what little coin he had in his possession.

Chester scrutinizes the journal, looking for dates. There are none though. For whatever reason, Geppetto has refrained from adding dates anywhere. Closing the book, he studies the title again. *Death of a Clown; Birth of an Artist.* Is the word *Death* metaphorical? He hopes so, for Chester knows without a shadow of doubt that the two of them are destined to meet. He pushes the thought of Geppetto's demise from his mind and imagines him living and breathing. What kind of artist did Geppetto become? It is not enough to read about his metamorphosis from clown to artist; Chester must see it for himself.

The practicalities of following in his tracks, terminating his employment and saying farewell to his family, do not enter his head. All he sees is a stranger who has transformed from clown to artist, one who holds the key to Chester being able to do the same. For the first time in ages, a weight has lifted.

The dimming room insists he pause and light a lamp. A glance at the clock tells him an hour or so remains until he will have to leave for the theatre. His heart plummets, knowing that Duke is likely to introduce him to the young protege who will have come to watch his every move. He cannot remember the lad's name, but he will need to be on top form tonight if he wants to impress him. On the other hand, what does it matter? He will be leaving for Italy soon, so if his performance is not up to scratch then so what. It does matter though. Chester has always been, and will in all likelihood remain, conscientious to a fault. The words the headmaster had written on Chester's graduation report feel burdensome now. *Conscientious to a fault.* Both he and his parents had been proud of the sentiment back then, but now those four words feel like a millstone around his neck.

Flicking the pages of the journal to determine how far he is likely to read before he needs to set off, he discovers to his dismay that the end of the chapter on Florence is, in fact, where the writing stops. Surely not! Chester turns page after page, searching for ink, but all he finds are blank sheets.

"No!" Chester's shout sends Arlo into a fit of pique. Jolted from sleep, the cat hisses like a snake and arches its back. Chester pays it no attention. Why for Cholly's sake has the writing come to such an abrupt end?

Chester paces the room, waving the journal like a weapon. Geppetto has filled him with hope, only to dash it by something mightier than the sword—the pen, or rather the lack of it. Is this some kind of ruse, a cruel trick to make him believe there is nothing better out there after all? Sensing Chester's mood, Arlo curls up small beneath a side table, watching him closely for signs of madness.

Chester slumps in the chair, sick to the stomach, and flicks from front to back one more time in the vain hope that some feat of magic will have conjured words that are presently invisible. He recalls the magician's face in the Reading Rooms, wondering if perhaps it was he who put the journal there for him to find. But of course such an idea makes no sense.

Less than five minutes ago he was planning his escape, to leave the city of his birth – his prison cell – and follow the footsteps of the clown known as Geppetto, a clown he already envisages in crisp clarity. How dare he trick him this way?

Cursing the clown to hell and back, he skips to the final page of writing. He skims the last paragraph, desperate for clues as to what went wrong. What he reads makes him shriek with joy and sends Arlo scarpering from beneath the table out to the tiny kitchen.

> *Our journey has come to an abrupt end, or so it would seem. Trust me when I say that it has not. In fact, it is just beginning. The answers you seek await you in Florence, at the Teatro Verdi, home of the Commedia dell'Arte!*
>
> *Come, be my honoured guest.*

3

O n Monday, their day of rest, Chester attends Mess for what he knows will be the last time. His travel ticket is booked; he leaves on Friday. His nerves are in tatters as he walks along Clown Alley, despite the skip in his step. He has been a clown for so long he does not think he is capable of walking in any other manner, at least not without making a conscious effort.

In the distance he spies The Sacred Church of Razzmatazz, bold red canopy above a black lacquered door, bright yellow walls, and slows his pace. He wishes to enter last so that he can sit at the back. That way, when the rest of the troupe flock out at the end of Mess, he can stay behind in order to speak with Father Roly. As much as he would like to pull a magician's trick and disappear into thin air, he believes he owes him this much. The man has been kind to him down the years, and besides, he hopes Father Roly will do him the favour of delivering a letter to his mother after he has fled.

The joyful sound of the brass band playing *Grand Marche Chromatique* reaches his ears at the foot of the steps, hastening him onward. Decorum is not the order of the day on the clown sabbath, in fact quite the opposite. Chester ducks to avoid a water fountain that is being squirted in jest from the gallery, all part of the proceedings, but he does not want to speak with Father Roly soaking wet.

Midwinter sunshine dances behind the stained-glass window of the King of Clowns, Joseph Grimaldi, making his dark eyes dance with glee at their antics. White face and pleated neck ruff, the King's gaze fixes on Chester, and in that moment he believes Grimaldi sees into his soul. Beneath the grease paint, Chester flushes.

The audience of clowns is in the throes of the welcome address. They stand in the pews, swaying to the rhythm of the brass band, their make-up and costumes a cornucopia of colour. On seeing him enter, one or two wave and beckon for him to sit with them, but Chester declines with a tilt of his hat and gestures at the back row where he blends among a few of the more sombre clowns. It has always been the way of things, Chester realizes. Those baptized into the Sacred Order of Tragicomedy have always veered more towards the edges than the centre.

He takes a deep breath and tries to immerse himself in the spirit of the ceremony but fails to do so. Instead of acting the fool, he wishes he could close his eyes and press his hands to his ears to drown out the sound of their raucous laughter and riotous antics. He is not mistaken; he does not belong here. A well of panic threatens to break through the surface, but his young protege, the Grim Peeper, has spied him from up in the gallery. The clownet waves frantically, as if he has been waiting for his hero to appear.

Chester manages a wink of kinship before feigning interest in the *Little Book of Nonsense* that sits in the slot in front of him.

A quiver of guilt in his stomach reminds him that he is about to let the child down badly.

The remainder of the service washes over him as he longs for it to end. A pinch of nostalgia is all he feels as one by one the clowns swagger from the church, slapping each other on the back and blowing horns in each other's faces, as is their way.

Chester grits his teeth and dons a fake smile, unable to comprehend how such eternal repetition does not douse their spirit. Instead, they thrive on it. He is certain the sameness feeds them with nectar, providing them the comfort of knowing they do not need to change, or develop, or think outside the box.

He watches from the window as Father Roly bids his flock farewell on the church steps, exchanging the odd act of mimicry and exaggerated expression with a few hangers on. Their images are distorted by the rippled glass, which adds to the overall sense of insanity.

Father Roly closes the door behind him and sighs as he enters the church, and for a moment Chester wonders if he, too, is glad that Mess is over.

"Ah, Chester," he says when he sees him. "I didn't realize you were still here." He tugs at his rainbow striped stole, as though nervous. Either that, or perhaps he was hoping to make a quick getaway, Chester thinks.

"May I have a word, Father?"

The minister frowns, and his white-caked make-up settles in the furrows. "Why of course."

Chester clears his throat in preparation for what he is about to say. "I'm leaving, Father." Beads of sweat burst through his skin, like miniature flower buds popping open. He swallows. "I wanted you to know, but I ask that you keep my confidence."

"Leaving? You mean the theatre, or London?"

"Yes...both." Chester whips out the envelope addressed to his mother and proffers it to Father Roly with a trembling hand. "I wonder if you'd be so kind as to give this to my mother once I'm gone." He shakes his head. "I-I'm afraid I don't have the courage to do so myself."

Father Roly takes the envelope from him and examines the name written thereon. He blinks successively, pencilled brows two boomerangs. "Well, of course, but don't you think it would be better coming from you?"

Chester shakes his head. "I-I can't."

"Well, in that case." Father Roly pockets the envelope and motions for Chester to be seated. "Do you want to talk? I'm all ears." He wiggles his white-gloved hands either side of his face and smiles, then takes up residence in the pew alongside Chester.

"It's just..." Chester pinches his lower lip. "I don't know where to start. Perhaps it's best if I come straight out with it."

Father Roly nods and waits.

"The truth is I've lost my faith, all of it. The constant glee, the pranks...everything about this life feels fake. I-I can't do it anymore." Chester removes his hat and rotates the brim round and round in his hands. Anything to avoid eye contact. He takes a deep breath. "Look, there's no easy way to say it. Truth is, I no longer wish to be a clown, and I no longer believe in Cholly." He senses Father Roly bristle.

Seconds tick away, then, with a sigh, Father Roly says, "Come with me. I want to show you something."

Father Roly gets to his feet and marches down the aisle. Chester follows, meek as a lamb. In front of the choir stalls he turns sharp left and enters a small room that Chester has never been in before. In comparison to the rest of the church, the room is simple and bare. No rainbows or paper streamers. No coloured glass or murals on the walls.

"Come in," Father Roly says, beckoning Chester inside. The minster gets on his knees and rolls a plain rug into a cylinder before sliding it out of the way. A trap door awaits. He unfastens the bolt then steps into the hole in the floor and disappears. "Well?" he calls. "You coming?"

Chester finds the whole thing bizarre but does as he is told and follows the minister into the crypt. Brick interior, encrusted with salt deposits that make the surface sparkle in the gloom. A vaulted ceiling from which an oil lamp is suspended. Father Roly lights the lamp and the space springs to life with moving shadows, both his and the minister's, as well as the pendulum on which the lamp hangs. The stone floor is pitted and cracked, but on closer inspection Chester sees that it is paved with gravestones, some of which are engraved with the names of the deceased. At the furthest end, a stone plinth, at approximate hip height juts from the wall. A wooden coffin rests upon it.

Father Roly turns to face Chester. "Do you scare easily?"

Chester shakes his head. "Not at the dead," he says, and his clouded breath meets the minister's in the middle and melds into one. "It's living that scares me."

Father Roly edges towards the coffin, taking care not to step on the grave-markers, then stops. "You question your faith and think us foolish," he says, a gloved hand resting on the wood. "We are who we are, Chester, and we cannot change that."

His tone suggests disapproval, and Chester almost wishes he had left without so much as a word. He takes a deep breath then says, "I must disagree with you, Father. I believe we can change, despite what you think. Yes, we are born and raised as clowns, but that does not mean we shouldn't seek a different way of life if it doesn't suit us, does it?"

The minister's eyes are arrowslits. "You think so? Well perhaps you'll feel differently once you've seen what I have to show you." He beckons Chester forward and opens the lid of the coffin. "Chester, meet our forefather and founder of this church." He unwraps a shroud, the colour of bone, and Chester finds himself looking down on a corpse.

But it is not really a corpse. It is nothing but a skeleton, all trace of the man of flesh removed by the bonds of time. Dark orbs, missing teeth, the skeleton wears a strange kind of grimace. At the centre of the skull is a spherical bony growth, unmistakably the nose of a clown.

"Do you see?" Father Roly says, his eyes glinting mischievously beneath the make-up. "This is your ancestor. There is no mistaking our identity, Chester. We are born with it and will keep it until our bones turn to dust."

Chester is lost for words. Never before has he seen a clown skeleton, not even in the form of a drawing. Why it should surprise him he does not know, and yet it does. The bulbous growth looks out of place, other-worldly almost. Without thinking, his hand goes to his own nose. He cossets the ball of cartilage in his palm, feeling its roundness.

Father Roly peels back the bottom half of the shroud. "And these," he says, pointing towards the feet. "Excuse the pun, but there's no escaping these either." His grin is that of a shark, sharp teeth and bloody gums, all the more prominent beneath his black-painted lips.

The skeleton's feet are huge. Six-inch metatarsals, phalanges tipped in the shape of mushrooms. Chester squirms, every bone in his own feet springing to life. *You see*, they seem to say, *there's no escaping us*. His feet are his enemy; they always have been. Even now they conspire against him and side with the minister. If Chester had an axe, he would chop them off right now and let Father Roly deal with the mess.

An overwhelming sense of dread swells in his chest. It is not the sight of the skeleton that causes him to feel faint but the feeling of being trapped in his own body.

"I have to go," he says, his hand a shield. "I trust you'll deliver the letter, Father." And with that he turns on his heels and rushes up the stairs as though the devil himself is after him.

Arlo is nowhere to be seen when he enters the flat. In his neighbour's, Lala Wiggins's, no doubt. The cat adores her. A ripple of guilt at the thought of abandoning Arlo, especially as it has not crossed his mind until now. Perhaps he should have a word, explain his intention and ask if Lala will look after Arlo if he offers to pay. He cannot though. Escaping is his secret, and confiding in another person would water it down like over-diluted cordial. Right now, he regrets telling Father Roly, too.

His notebook is open on the desk. Chester submits to the only form of escapism he knows—the world that appears at the end of his pen.

The City of Silence
by Runo Quill

The Emperor decreed that henceforth there would be no more questions.

"I'm sorry, Your Majesty," said the Duke. "I do not understand your meaning. Could you explain a little clearer?"

The Emperor glared at the Duke with such ferocity that the Duke recoiled. "That is precisely the reason for the decree. Questions, questions, so many questions!" Flared nostrils, breath of a dragon, the Duke feared that should the Emperor open his mouth to speak again he would be scorched by the flames. He took a step back. "B-but who do you mean, Your Majesty? Do you mean that none of us shall be permitted to ask a question of *you*?"

The Emperor gripped the edge of the desk so that the bones of his knuckles shone white. He ground his teeth, and as he spoke, spittle flew, dousing the flames beneath the Emperor's words. "Fool! Let me spell it out for you. I mean that from now on questions of any kind are prohibited in the whole of the kingdom. No one, from the youngest child to the oldest citizen, is permitted to ask a question of anyone ever again."

The Duke trembled from head to toe. "But, Your Majesty, how do you intend to enforce such a thing? I mean, we cannot have spies all over the city. How will we know what our subjects say to one another in their own homes?"

The Emperor leapt to his feet and swiped the contents of his desk to the floor. "You, fool, have already broken the decree by asking such a thing! We will enforce it by whatever means necessary, and furthermore, the city walls will be inscribed with a list of words that are banned from this day forth, starting with the word *Why*, since it is the word I detest most."

The Duke, conceding defeat, bowed his head and folded his hands in a prayer like manner. "Yes, Your Majesty. I will see it is done."

So the Duke consulted with the barons, and the barons consulted with the noblemen, and the noblemen called forth a team of stonemasons and assembled them in front of the city gates.

The nobleman in charge gestured towards the city walls. "Stonemasons, you are to inscribe in these stones words that may be classed as interrogations, starting with the most obvious—*Why, Who, Where, How* etcetera, and we will add to them as we see fit. Do you understand?"

"And to what purpose, might I ask?" said the Head of the Guild.

"No, you may not," replied the nobleman. "And if you ask again, you will be punished. Now pick up your tools and set to work." The nobleman thrust a handwritten list at the Head of the Guild and walked away with his nose held high.

And so it began. The stonemasons carved a word in each stone that made up the city walls, starting at the front of the gates and working in a clockwise fashion in the trajectory of the sun.

Meanwhile, the people of the city were called to a meeting, a meeting of fundamental importance which no one was spared from attending, even if sick or about to give birth.

They were told of the new decree, and also that should the rule be broken they would be punished.

Questions danced on every tongue. Questions such as why the rule had come into existence and how it might be enforced. Questions such as who would enforce the rule, and what might happen if it were broken. But not one of them was brave enough, or foolish enough, to allow the question to spill from their lips.

The Archduke was the only person with enough courage to speak with the Emperor about the decree, and even he chose his words carefully.

"I was thinking, Your Majesty...perhaps we should give our citizens time to adjust, a few weeks, say, a month at most. You see, to alter one's way of thinking, and therefore speaking, is a slow process. Your subjects will need time to consider the words they want to say before verbalizing them. If we are too hasty with our punishment, it might spark a revolution."

The Emperor grunted and grumbled, but he had to acquiesce that such a change would require a great deal of thought. And that was precisely his thinking. You see, he believed that the more conscious his people became of their words, the less likely they were to make ridiculous demands of him as emperor. He also knew they would be less likely to speak, and that fear of reprisal would mean a more subservient population.

"I'll grant them two weeks and not a day longer," he said. His cunning plan was that given time the people would grow so frustrated by having to consider every word, they would stop speaking altogether. Then he would rule over the most docile and subservient people in all the world.

As for the punishment, for each question asked, a stitch would be inserted in the lip, starting from the corner of the mouth and working towards the centre. The stitch would be sewn with the strongest fishing gut available and would be permanent. A record for each citizen would be kept at the palace to ensure no one removed his or her stitches. Each slip-up would result in a new stitch, until eventually the whole of their mouths would be sewn together. Then, without the ability to eat or drink, they would die. This, he believed, should be enough of a threat to keep them on their toes.

He planned to reinforce his scheme through a system of reward, with each man, woman and child responsible for betraying his or her friends or family in order to claim a reward in the form of a gold coin. Except the coins would not be made of real gold but fool's gold, which could be traded not only for necessities but also for the worthless nonsense sold within the city that they seemed so addicted to.

He was certain over time the population would become as malleable as soft clay. Then, he could mould them into shape and bake them dry.

The Emperor's plan worked. Each day, new forbidden words were added to the city walls. The list expanded to include any kind of interrogative form of a word, even those most commonly spoken, such as *is* or *were,* if used in the form of a question. Even the Archduke received a stitch when he accidentally broke the law.

"Are you happy with the way things are progressing?" he asked the Emperor over lunch, and was swiftly administered a stitch by the Emperor's own physician, who himself had received three stitches the previous week for enquiring as to the Emperor's health.

Within the first few weeks, many citizens received stitches in their lips, and mumbling became the new norm.

In fact, within a month or two very few lips remained unstitched, and conversation grew more and more stilted.

Over time, the city grew increasingly silent. The people were tricked into believing they were better off, having traded free speech for material wealth. Indeed, they were able to purchase more goods with their fake coins, but they did not stop to consider the fact that since it was the Emperor who owned the shops by spending their coins they were, in fact, giving him back his wealth.

As for the Emperor, the less they questioned the more they accepted, and the more they accepted the less they questioned, which was precisely his intention from the outset.

So let this act as a warning. Should you happen upon the City of Silence, do not enquire as to why its citizens race round in circles purchasing items they do not need, most of which they will never use. And do not question the mumbling way in which they speak, because if you do you will find yourself with a stitch in your lip.

4

The sky is ink black when Chester gets out of bed on Friday morning. Arlo stirs, arches his back, then tiptoes over to where Chester stands in front of the window and leaps into his arms. Chester strokes Arlo's soft fur, and the cat purrs. "The time has come for us to say goodbye, Arlo." The words tighten his throat in their vice-like grip. "I hope you'll forgive me." Arlo rubs his face against Chester's stubble and closes his eyes so that Chester cannot see the hurt that lies therein. He pours milk into Arlo's dish and watches the pink tongue lap.

Chester is well prepared. His bags are packed, and an envelope addressed to his neighbour, Lala Wiggins, waits on the countertop. Half past five, according to the bedside clock. She will be fast asleep, so the sound of the envelope dropping onto her mat should not wake her.

Once dressed, he cannot bear to say goodbye to Arlo, who having drunk the milk has retired back to bed, so he picks up his suitcase and heads out the door. The only guilt he carries has Arlo's name written on it. No remorse for not having said goodbye to family or friends. No qualm about leaving his job, but to abandon an animal is wrong. He carries the burden of it between his ribs.

Late winter air steals his breath as he opens the door. He welcomes its slap in the face, accepting it as punishment for abandoning Arlo. A full moon casts a silver light on the icy cobbles, warning him to tread carefully. Chester is grateful for the stillness. Each breath he releases is a ghost at his shoulder. A ghost of a past life, soon to be resurrected in its new form.

He passes the school and The Sacred Church of Razzmatazz, shuddering as he recalls the clown skeleton in the crypt. Far more frightening, though, are Father Roly's words. *There is no mistaking our identity, Chester. We are born with it and will keep it until our bones turn to dust.*

Chester is determined to prove him wrong. In fact, he will prove them all wrong.

At the crossroads between Clown Quarter and Magician's Quarter he takes the first coach of the day, hoping it will get him to Crystal Palace railway station in time for the seven o'clock train to Kent.

"Going to the exhibition?" the driver asks as Chester pays him the penny for his journey.

"No, I'm taking a train to Kent."

The driver's attention is diverted towards a young woman who is struggling with her skirts. "Allow me to take that for you, Ma'am," he says, lifting the woman's travel case and holding out his other hand to assist her up the steps.

Chester is glad of the distraction and waits for the woman to mount the carriage before following suit and securing his suitcase to the overhead luggage rack. The carriage seats eight, but so far, he and the woman are the only customers. He wonders why she is travelling alone at such an early hour and, as usual, is acutely aware of his nose and feet. He has dressed as formally as his wardrobe would allow—black wide-leg trousers and jacket, white shirt, and of course his overcoat and wide-brimmed hat, and yet he knows his clownish features mark him out.

The woman pays him no attention but clutches her purse tight and gazes out of the window at a sky suggestive of night rather than day. If only she knew, Chester thinks. He is far more apprehensive than she is.

With a sudden lurch that turns what is left of Chester's internal organs to jelly, the coach pulls off, and rumbles down a road that glistens with frost. He settles in his seat and closes his eyes, tuning in to the clip clop of the horses' hooves in an effort to quell his nerves. Once around the next corner, it will be the furthest away from home he has ever been. What a sheltered life he has led. A life without ambition, until now.

As dawn breaks on the horizon, the city wakes. Street-sellers set up their stalls, young boys push handcarts laden with goods, lamplighters on ladders extinguish the streetlights. It is as if an invisible being has set off a silent alarm clock and shaken the city awake.

With each stop the carriage makes, customers alight, shivering as they step into the frosty air, while those boarding are grateful for the warm ghosts they leave in their wake. And still the young woman does not move. If anything, she grips her purse tighter, her gaze ever outward towards the streets, and Chester wonders if perhaps he was wrong in thinking her less anxious than him.

As the Crystal Palace comes into view, Chester's attention is directed towards it. A glass palace fit for a queen. And yet it is not. He has read about it in the papers and knows it is a place of learning, a place that attracts visitors from all over the world. A wave of regret at not having visited it sweeps over him. He knows that once away from London he will never return. He will not make the same mistake as Zar did in his story *The Raven and the Tightrope Walker,* so he will never get to see inside the Palace. So mesmerized is he by the crystal structure that he almost forgets he has reached his destination. He grabs his suitcase with a flurry and disembarks.

"Which way to the station?" he calls to the driver.

"Straight on down the road, then left as soon as you see the lake."

Chester tips his hat and sets off, adjusting his stride to mimic the other pedestrians. No splayed feet or duck waddle, no pausing to cartwheel down the road or grab buns from a street-seller and juggle them, even though his excitement urges him to. *This whole trip is about losing your clownishness,* he reminds himself, so why does he feel a spontaneous urge to pull tricks?

Early morning light reflects on the lake in the distance, turning its surface into a gigantic mirror, one which makes him reflect on his feelings. He is confused as to his own motives. The life of a clown may be defined as a form of escapism from the harsh reality of life, and yet it has become his anathema, and as such has had the opposite effect.

The train whistles its way out of the station, and Chester peers from the window as passengers vacate the platform and head for the stairs that will lead them into the vast arms of the city. A train passing in the opposite direction makes him start. He presses his hands to his ears to drown out the noise. Despite being over six foot tall, he feels as small and vulnerable as a child. Never before has he taken a train, never mind a ferry to another country.

Chester leans back in the seat and tries to relax, grateful that there is just one other passenger in his coach, a gentleman who sits on the opposite side with his head in a newspaper.

The city thins and suburbs thrive. Grey skyline gives way to green as the train journeys south through Sevenoaks and ever on towards the sea.

The gentleman who shared Chester's coach disembarks soon afterwards, leaving behind his copy of The Westminster Gazette, so Chester picks it up and pretends to read as other passengers come and go. The newspaper offers nothing of interest, but it serves as a screen behind which to hide. He peeps from behind its pages, considering the lives and destinations of his fellow passengers. *Do they wonder about me?* he thinks, though few pay him more than a cursory glance, and for this he is grateful.

Chester smells the briny tang of the English Channel before he sees it. He folds the paper and places it on the rack above his head, retrieving his suitcase at the same time. Admiralty Pier stretches one long arm out into the sea in its effort to stem the tide. The train judders to a halt and waits until a Stirling engine passes the signal box before resuming its journey, coughing and spluttering as it picks up speed.

Despite the early hour, the harbour is bustling. An arrangement of boats and ships are dotted about the water with no apparent order, and yet there must be, Chester thinks, or else the smaller boats would come to harm. An enormous paddle steamer butts up against the Pier wall, both funnels oozing steam and smoke in equal measure.

Chester alights into a world that smells both of the sea and burning coal. The hairs on his arms stand proud as a wave of excitement courses through him. And the noise! Bells and whistles, horns and voices, unfamiliar tongues.

A glance at the station clock informs him he has more than an hour to spare before boarding, so Chester considers how best to pass the time. Instinct suggests he finds a quiet corner and whiles it away by people watching; his stomach suggests otherwise. Only now does he realize he has eaten nothing since the previous evening. Taking a deep breath, he heads for a nearby inn in the hope of catching some breakfast. *If you are to travel the world and throw off your bounds, you will need to engage with all kinds of people,* he tells himself with more conviction than he feels.

As he heads towards the row of shops and cafes on the seafront, he summons to mind Geppetto, the man whose voice rings loud and clear in Chester's ears, even though he has never heard him speak. The journal is sufficient to glean that Geppetto is made of far sterner stuff than he. Confident, unafraid, and yet Chester wonders if he too felt apprehensive at the start of his journey. Did he while away the time here as Chester is doing? Were his nerves in tatters, like Chester's?

Ensconced in the bay window of an inn called The First and Last, he orders a pot of tea and a bowl of cream and wheat and watches the comings and goings of the harbour.

With twenty minutes to spare, he pays the bill and heads towards the ferry, knowing that soon he will leave English soil, never to return. He swallows hard, certain that by now his neighbour, Lala Wiggins, will have read the note. No doubt she will relish the opportunity to tittle-tattle, but as long as she welcomes Arlo he does not care.

Chester's knees threaten to give way as he climbs aboard the ferry. His mouth runs dry; his chest tightens. He stands on deck, gripping the rail. Facing the chalk-white cliffs, he slips Geppetto's journal from his overcoat pocket, seeking reassurance that the journey he is embarking on is the right one. He turns to the final paragraph.

> *Are you ready?* The words say...*We begin in Florence, Italy, the place where The Story of a Puppet was written and the place I escaped to first.*

With a nod of certainty, he pockets the book and wraps his coat around his middle. The tea and oatmeal have warmed his insides, but the wind that blows from France is far from welcoming. Refusing to see it as a portent of things to come, he fixes his gaze on the white cliffs and bids them farewell.

Beneath his breath he mutters words of great significance to him, words that would mean nothing to a passing stranger who happened to catch them. Only the seagulls seem to register their meaning, as they take to the air with a high-pitched squawk of indifference.

"I leave behind the chalk-white face, both yours and mine forever," he says, and in his heart he means it.

5

B y the time Chester's train arrives at Paris, dusk has fallen, and the bustling station is cast in the golden glow of row upon row of gas lamps. He alights, stopping to marvel at the majesty of the station. Glass ceilings and iron architecture covers the tracks of what can only be described as an enormous central hall, one which despite the noise and crowds feels vast, a world within a world.

His ears are assaulted by shrill whistles and the hiss of steam, his nose by the acrid tang of smoke. A passing guard announces the arrival of the train to Orléans, and Chester repeats the words under his breath, relishing in the rolling trill of the *r* sounds, the lilting edge of the vowels.

The motion of the ferry and the long train journey causes him to sway a little, and when at last he moves towards the exit his legs wobble. Though eager to reach Florence, Chester decides he will stay in Paris for the night and continue his journey tomorrow.

Home, he thinks, realizing he instinctively considered London as such when he contemplated Geppetto's journey. And yet his heart insists otherwise. When he thinks of home, he envisages his apartment and Arlo, nothing or no one else. How long will it take for his psyche to shake off the old notion of home and adapt to a new one? Will he ever feel at home again, or is he destined to search the world for something that does not truly exist?

He shakes his head to clear himself of negative thoughts and steps into a rain-soaked street. Unlike the clear blue skies of his departure, a blanket of cloud has descended on the city, obliterating the early evening stars and giving the busy street the illusion of looking through an unfocussed lens. Yet it does nothing to dampen his spirit.

The street is lined with shops and kiosks, most of which are in the process of closing for the day. A Parfumerie window displays twinkling glass bottles with floral labels, and on the corner a Tabac selling evening newspapers and an array of pipes, snuff jars and tobacco tins. He takes a deep breath before entering.

An elderly gentleman behind the counter glances over his spectacles, and Chester prepares to speak.

"*Bonsoir, Monsieur.*"

The man returns the greeting, and Chester is lost for words. French words, at least.

"Do you know where I might find lodging for the night? A hotel, perhaps?"

The man flutters a hand towards the door. "*Ah, oui oui.*"

What follows is a blend of French and English and several gestures, from which Chester gleans the name of two hotels that by all accounts are within walking distance. As a gesture of gratitude, he purchases an evening newspaper with the few centimes he has in his pocket, knowing he will hardly be able to read a word, then doffs his hat and leaves, taking the scent of tobacco with him.

That wasn't so bad, he thinks as he crosses the busy street. At least he had found the confidence to interact, and he had been so busy deciphering the Tabac owner's instructions he had forgotten about his hideous nose and long feet.

Before the persistent drizzle has a chance to soak through Chester's overcoat, he secures lodging for the night in a boarding house on the Rue de Maubeuge. Tomorrow he will cross country and take a train to Switzerland, but for now he is content with the warmth of his room and a supper of bouillabaisse, bread, and a bottle of Chateau Margaux to wash it down. Chester rarely partakes of alcohol, so by the time he has finished the stew his face is flushed and his tongue loosened to the point of conversing with the waiter.

During the meal he considers how he would love to visit the cathedral of Notre Dame before leaving, as Victor Hugo's novel, *The Hunchback of Notre Dame*, has haunted his thoughts since he first read it during his late teens. Perhaps he could book a sleeper to Switzerland instead of travelling by day. He had wanted to see as much of the countryside as possible and had therefore intended to travel during daylight, but the cathedral is too appealing to miss.

By the time his head hits the pillow, he has made up his mind. He will book a sleeper for the following evening and visit Notre Dame in the morning.

The day dawns full of promise, the act of waking in an unfamiliar room, in an unfamiliar country, fills Chester with delight, not dread. Having booked his ticket for the sleeper, he leaves his luggage at the hotel and makes his way towards Notre Dame on the Ile de la Cité, some two miles distant.

This is the first day he has spent outside of London, and already it feels like a re-birth. No one knows him here. He can be whomever he wants and go wherever he chooses. Unrestricted. Untethered. A new man in a new world. His stride is confident. Today, Chester does his best to hold his head high instead of peering from beneath the rim of his hat. He catches the eye of a few passers-by, certain they do not flinch or gaze at his features any longer than is proper. He listens as they pass him by, in case one of them should turn and stare at the back of a tall man, dressed in black, with enormous feet. But they do not.

It is with this new-found confidence that he arrives in front of the building that has stolen into his dreams for more than a decade. Breathtaking. As the bells chime the hour, the hair on his arms stands erect. Little wonder they rendered Quasi-modo deaf. It is thanks to Hugo's great novel that this build-ing is restored, for having fallen into disrepair the book re-newed interest in its fate. How different it looks to The Sa-cred Church of Razzmatazz, the only other religious building he has ever stepped foot inside. Subtle grey stone instead of brightly coloured brick. Twin towers, arched windows, and if he squints skyward, he is able to make out the gargoyles and chimera on the turrets. The mythical monsters whose heads are nailed in place to serve as water fountains. He knows many of them by name, for they have always fascinated him. Wyvern, the two-footed dragon, and the playful Stryga who wears a bored expression and pokes out his tongue. The one-horned demon, the goat-human hybrid, the plucky heron. Chester hopes to be able to see at least some of them up close, for they feel like old acquaintances.

According to legend, Notre Dame is said to be home to the revered crown of thorns, as well as a fragment of the wooden cross and a nail from the Holy Sepulchre. Quite a contrast to the bony skeleton presented to Chester at his own church. But it is not for religious purposes that Chester admires this place. In truth, were it not for Hugo's novel, he would probably not have visited.

He pauses at the entrance, his eyes searching for the wooden shelf where Quasimodo's father left him as a baby, but he cannot locate it. Once inside, however, he forgets the hunchback's fate for a while, such is the magnificence of the place. A columned nave stretches into the far distance. The smell of incense, and a chorus of unseen voices. Disembodied angels that fill the space to the rafters with song. It sends a shiver down Chester's spine. How can anyone fail to be moved by such a spectacle? This early in the day there are few visitors, and the few who are here have fallen under the same spell and do not speak.

Chester spends an hour at the cathedral, then another on the banks of La Seine, browsing the book stalls and stopping at a little café. He sits in the shadow of the canal wall, looking back towards Notre Dame with its twin towers and heavenward spire, upon which sits a copper rooster, and imagines poor Quasimodo raised within those walls. He understands why he is drawn to such a character. Though ugly on the outside, Quasimodo is kind at heart, and astutely aware of the extent to which society is fooled by outward appearance.

The Cathedral bells toll eleven, ample time to spare. Chester slips his notebook from his pocket and begins to write.

The Three Lives of Quasimodo

By Runo Quill

Very few realize my birth name was Lapis, not Quasimodo. Lessons learned during my first life serve me well, for in this life I have not repeated those grave errors of judgement. *Trust no-one and you will not be disappointed* ranks high on the list.

Legend has it that I was born to the Roma, but that is untrue. Allow me to explain...

My father was a sculptor, one of several employed to produce gargoyles for the cathedral of Notre Dame. He was a true artist who loved his work, but he was also crippled by loneliness.

This is the story he told me when I was but a young child, and I believe it to this day.

Having sculpted my brother, Styrga, Father turned his attention to me. Thoughts bleak, spirit a black void, his intention was to sculpt a gargoyle the likes of which had never been seen before. A monster with semi-human features, one that would incite both loathing and pity in those who encountered it. Suffice it to say, he achieved more than he imagined.

Having half completed the task, he retired to bed with a heavy heart. Lonely, contemplative, embroiled in self-pity. That night, instead of kneeling before a Christian god, he knelt before the old gods, praying they might guide him or at least offer him respite from his morbid thoughts. In his right hand he held his favourite carving chisel; in his left a thorny acanthus leaf which he had been studying so that he might adorn the base of my brother's sculpture with a stone version of the same. The acanthus leaf: symbol of pain, sin, and punishment for Christians, but the symbol of enduring life in ancient lore.

When the cold light of dawn broke, he woke to the smell of sun-kissed stone and the sound of a baby's cry. The first he was familiar with, the second not so. He pulled on his trousers and followed the haunting cry all the way to his workshop.

Expecting to see the half-finished sculpture atop the bench, he was astonished to discover a basket, woven from the deep-lobed leaves of the acanthus plant, its foliage dark and bold. Inside, beneath a makeshift blanket sprinkled with the muted purple petals of the acanthus flower, lay my naked form. The sight that greeted him as he peeled back the blanket caused his old heart to sink. No neck separated my head from my shoulders, and my breastbone protruded as though some alien creature lurked beneath, waiting to burst forth.

Twisted legs kicked the air, balled fists rammed inside a cavernous mouth which drooled saliva. My left eye watched Father, while my right, distorted by a warty growth, faced towards the door through which he had entered.

Father said that in that moment he knew I had been sent by the gods to test the depth of his sorrow, but despite knowing this, he spent a minute or so trying to locate the half-finished sculpture he had carved the previous night.

Realizing his prayers had been answered, albeit in a strange fashion, his compassion was ignited, and at that moment he made a silent vow to raise me as his own.

He named me Lapis, Latin for stone, but also because my eyes were deep blue pools that leaked a constant trickle.

I remember almost nothing of the first four years of life. If I focus hard, I can recall Father's face: a kindly expression behind eyes that knew pain, a road map of lines and wrinkles that spoke of hardship but little else. Until the day he delivered me to the foundling.

By then I had grown into my skin, my deformity more pronounced with each passing year. Spine a twisted corkscrew and hunched to match the bulge at the front at my chest rendered each loping step agony. And my face: jagged teeth protruded tusk-like over the bottom lip while the wen that covered my right eye forced the lid half-open both day and night, so that it appeared as though I never slept. Most noticeable of all was the melancholic expression which refused to budge no matter how I contorted my face. Maybe I foresaw the path ahead, even as an infant.

Father lay me down on a wooden bed, walled into the porch of the Cathedral. I remember the words he spoke, his voice choked with emotion. "Lapis," he said, "I am dying and therefore must entrust you to the hands of the church and hope they will do that which is good and right." His voice broke and a tear slid down his cheek.

I raised a finger and wiped the tear away.

"Know that you have brought me more joy these past four years than ever I knew before," he said, and with that he limped into the darkness without so much as a backward glance. And I was left with only the image of St. Christopher and the statue of Antoine the Knight to watch over me.

The rest, as they say, is history.

I shall not dwell on how Archdeacon Frollo changed my name to Quasimodo, meaning *something half formed*, nor shall I speak of the torturous treatment waiting in the wings. I am certain you will have heard the tale many times, and it is not my intention to bore you. Suffice it to say that the mark of difference was, and to this day remains, an excuse to mistreat its victims.

Instead, I shall skip to the end and back again, for it is true that when she died I followed Esmerelda to the vault at Montfaucon. True that I lay entwined in her lifeless arms, head pressed to a bosom that failed to rise or fall, kissed lips blue as forget-me-nots, all of which I had failed to accomplish while she was alive.

Hunger and thirst became the tormentor, cold the inter-rogator, but not once did I stray from her side. Our bodies decayed as one; bones crumbled to dust at the hands of those who eventually found us.

All except for my heart. For that was made of stone. The one piece of me that still belonged to Father. Deep inside the core it beat an undetectable pulse of life, granted by the old gods. Of course, those who found it assumed my heart to be another rock within the tomb and left it there, undisturbed.

How wrong they were.

Do not believe what is said about the heart being the centre of emotion, for it is untrue. While we may sense the repercussion of abuse and cruelty as a quickening of the heart, it is merely an auto response. The essence of a person goes far deeper.

Some time later my heart of stone was plucked from the tomb by an immortal hand and taken to a secret wooded glade, far, far from the city. Here I was granted rest, my heart of stone wrapped in a blanket of sphagnum moss and cocooned in a snow goose's nest before being hidden in the trunk of a red oak, hollowed with age.

Five hundred years I slept, four times longer than Grimm's Sleeping Beauty, and as I slept I dreamed of Father's gnarled hands and Esmerelda's rosebud lips, the scent of lavender and the distant peal of bells. And all the while a kindly voice whispered on the wind: "When you are ready, son...When you are ready."

On the eve of the new millennia, I found myself on the Champ de Mars toasting the world with the words, *Bonne année*, and a glass of cheap Bordeaux. Twenty years old, the same age I had been when my first life ended, and christened René, meaning reborn. At first I had no recollection of my former life.

Until I visited Notre Dame.

I stood hands on hips before her majesty, shielding my eyes from the sun and gazing in awe at her magnificent towers. The bells tolled, their haunting peal welcoming me back into the flock, and in that moment I remembered. My brother Wyverne, the two-legged dragon, beat his wings in a flurry of excitement whilst my sister, the heron, croaked a frenzied cry of welcome.

I was home.

No longer a bellringer, instead I wait tables at La Maison Rose in the district of Montmartre by day, make props for the little theatre in the Cité Véron at night, and visit Notre Dame as often as I can.

Lulled into a false sense of security, I thought the world had changed, that in over half a century great progress had been made and lessons learned. It did not take long to discover this is not the case.

Like a wolf in sheep's clothing, the city's outward demeanour speaks of civility.

Buildings change, technology progresses, but people do not change. Still, they fear difference and grow intolerant of those who are unlike themselves. Since my return I have witnessed so much anger, so much pain, that I now believe real change is hopeless, that mankind will destroy itself first.

Nothing has changed. The wolf delivers the same bite. His coat may be shinier, but his teeth are just as sharp.

6

It is not until the train is crossing the Alps that the ridiculousness of Chester's situation hits. Mid-morning, and the sky is a vivid blue tarpaulin with only the sun for company. This high up, he feels as though he could reach out an arm and touch it. Surrounded by snow-capped jagged peaks, beneath which lush green mountains are dotted with matchbox buildings, Chester believes himself shrunk to the size of an ant. How insignificant he is. How unimportant.

His head swims and his heart palpitates. Fearing he might faint, he squeezes his eyes shut tight and utters a prayer to The Clown God, Cholly, in whom he no longer believes. It is not the great height that terrifies him, but the sudden realization of being so far from home, with no real plan for the future. Chester, a clown who until now has been in the habit of planning every minor detail, is lost in an unfamiliar world, alone. The journal could be a trick, a plant by some wicked magician to throw him off course. Geppetto might be nothing more than a fictitious sprite.

The gentleman sitting opposite raises a brow. "Are you all right? Can I get you something?"

Chester takes several deep breaths before answering. "I'm fine, thanks. A headache, that's all."

"It's the altitude," the man says. "The air's rather thin this high up."

Chester's fingers tingle, so he clenches and unclenches them several times in an attempt to bring them back to life. The last thing he feels like is small talk, so he closes his eyes, imagining the man's eyes boring into him. If he could wave a wand and be right back in his apartment he would do so.

Once he has calmed, he retrieves Geppetto's journal from his pocket and reads from beginning to end. This is why he is here. This, and nothing else.

By the time the train arrives in Turin, Chester is feeling far more positive. Clean, crisp air and the aroma of freshly brewed coffee greets him as he exits the station. He heads for the nearest *pasticceria* and orders strong black coffee and a raspberry pastry, delighting in the ensuing caffeine and sugar rush. From the patio table at which he sits, the snow-capped Alps are visible in the distance, making the twilit city blush pink with pride. Never has he witnessed such a sight. Low lying London rarely sees snow, and the only mountains are those he must climb in order to escape the place. He will spend the night here and take an early train to Florence tomorrow instead. After all, there is a place in Turin he would very much like to visit.

Via Carlo Alberto with its elegant arcades and arched windows was once home to one of Chester's favourite thinkers—Friedrich Nietzsche. Chester cranes his neck to view the second-storey window, the shutters of which are wide open despite the nip in the air. He imagines the philosopher leaning out and watching the comings and goings of the city. But it is also the last place Nietzsche lived before his breakdown and subsequent return to Germany. This is the place in which he wrote *Ecce Homo*, his autobiography. Aside from Geppetto's journal it is the last book Chester read prior to his epiphany. Is it in part responsible for Chester's radical actions? He ponders the question as he stands on the street corner. It is possible, since the work is at heart about the philosopher's inner struggles. Was the text also instrumental in Chester's denial of the Great God Cholly? Possibly.

And yet Chester is his own man, it is just that having had his eyes opened he finds it impossible to close them again.

He has spent a great deal of time considering the writing of Nietzsche and admits to finding it difficult to understand. He has also considered the man's fate, his sudden and tragic decline, which was reported to have occurred right here, in this part of the city. If Nietzsche has taught him anything it is that free will does not exist, or at least not in the metaphysical sense. The only thing he can do is follow his heart and hope to find a sense of purpose. But Nietzsche would argue against that sentiment, too, since he believed hope only prolongs torment.

Chester wanders the city streets, enjoying the serenity and calm. He remembers wandering into Magician's Quarter back home, his head bowed low and stride uncertain. Already he feels more confident, more assertive. Why, now and then he is able to look people in the eye and smile. Can so much change be affected over such a short period of time?

Soon he draws close to Regio, the famous royal theatre, and studies the billboard. This evening's opera is none other than Strauss's *Salome*, but the performance begins in one hour. Chester recalls the plot, having read it during one of his secret sojourns to the Reading Rooms. The story tells of Herod's stepdaughter, Salome, who requests the head of John the Baptist be served on a plate. He pictures Caravaggio's painting, remembering how unmoved Salome appears in the scene, and the executioner, too. A man who does what those who are rich and powerful ask of him without question or morals. It was the old woman in the background, her wraithlike presence, the detail of her face, that captured his attention, more so even than the decapitated head of the Baptist.

Chester enters the theatre with his fingers crossed behind his back in the hope that there might be a spare ticket.

The journey to Florence takes all of five hours, including a changeover in Milan and another at Bologna, giving Chester plenty of time to think. The railway line splices through sparsely occupied verdant land before giving way to dramatic scenery and snaking rivers as it journeys through Lombardy, and yet in truth he notices little. For most of the journey his thoughts turn inward to both analyse and rationalize his reasons for fleeing everything and everyone he has ever known.

Yes, he no longer wishes to be a clown, of that he is certain, but couldn't he have simply left the theatre and found something else to do closer to home?

Deep down, he knows this would have been impossible. The familial and peer pressure to stay within the fold, to remain entrenched in what everyone around him perceived as the truth, would have been too great. He needed to get away from all that his old life encompassed.

Chester preoccupies himself with the notion of communication and all that it entails. In truth, spoken communication is not his forte. His role as a tragic clown requires little in the way of debate or verbal expression and has far more to do with non-verbal communication. And his family and friends, too. They thrive on foolery and fun, not debate or discussion, since it saves them from thinking too deeply. However, that does not stop them from being opinionated. It also enables them to reinforce the belief that only those things they gain pleasure from are worthy of pursuit. They do not realize this though, of that Chester is certain, for they never analyse it. What would the great thinkers make of their simple acceptance?

There are many reasons why Chester lacks confidence in his ability to converse on a deep level, and lack of experience is one of them. Not so inwardly, though, for his mind is always active, ever ready to participate in the next debate, the next round of analysis. There does, however, seem to be a barrier between what happens inside his head and what his lips are capable of producing. A physical barring of the transposition between thought and speech, which is frustrating to say the least.

He will start small, as he has done so far on this journey, and take it from there. And in any case, the language barrier will prevent him from having to communicate on too high a level. Take last night's opera experience for example. He had managed to purchase a last-minute aisle seat up in the gods and had found himself next to a rotund Italian whose only acknowledgement of Chester's existence had been to ask that he move for him to visit the gents during the interval. Even he had seemed to infer by some unspoken means that Chester was not, in fact, Italian, as he had pointed towards the sign and waved his hand instead of speaking.

What is it about people, Chester wonders, that allows them to gleam so much about a person without the need for any kind of conversation? His pale complexion might suggest he hails from somewhere north of Italy, but his mode of dress is like any other. While his nose and feet mark him out as a clown, there is little else to suggest he is English. Would he have known the gentleman to be of Italian descent had he not been in Italy? Chester thinks about this and concludes that yes, the olive-toned skin, dark eyes and short stature might have given him cause to guess. Anthropology...a fascinating subject, and one Chester would like to study in the future. Ah, if only his brothers could hear his thoughts now.

Teatro Verdi, the theatre Geppetto summoned him to, is situated down a narrow street, flanked by restaurants and bars, all of which are built of sun-baked stone with shuttered windows, painted brown. As Chester looks upward his shoulders compress, such is the feeling of claustrophobia. The buildings stare down at him, threatening to collapse should he be audacious enough to criticize their great height in such a narrow street. Who am I to criticize anyone's height? he thinks. What did he expect the theatre to look like? An imposing visage on the corner of a busy junction perhaps, a renaissance masterpiece, complete with columns and arches, opposite a lawned park with flower beds. Not this. Anything but this. Ah well, at least its name is lettered in gold.

He takes a deep breath and enters, though this early in the afternoon no performance is running. Despite the building's disappointing facade, the interior is far more lavish, with marbled floors and an ornate box office smothered in posters of actors, singers and such like. Chester scans the black and white images, hoping to see one of a clown with the name Geppetto written underneath.

The box office is shuttered, and a sign reads: *Aperto dalle cinque alle diec.* His understanding of Italian is sufficient to allow him to guess that opening hours are from five o'clock until ten, though in order to determine this he finds it necessary to recite the numbers under his breath while counting on his fingers.

He glances at the clock. Ten past two. He cannot wait three more hours without asking if anyone remembers Geppetto. If no one is here, then why is the building open? Chester paces the foyer like a caged lion, hoping someone might appear. To his left, a sweeping staircase with marble steps and gold handrails rises; to his right, a door reads *Bancarelle* which he assumes means *Stalls.* He covers the space in four paces but is disappointed to find the door locked. A janitor would do, anyone would be better than no one. In his head, he repeats the line he has prepared over and over, like a mantra. Though simple in construction, it is the most his grasp of Italian will allow him before he will need to revert to the mother tongue, and even now he is not confident it is correctly translated. *"Scusa, conosci Geppetto?"* Without the Italian dictionary tucked inside his coat pocket, he would not have been able to formulate even this.

The longer he waits, the more nervous he grows until the back of his neck aches and his hands sweat profusely. Should he leave and come back at opening time? Now that he is here, he cannot bear the thought of waiting three more hours.

Deciding to chance his luck, he turns to face the stairs, hoping someone might be in the circle, cleaning perhaps. Surely someone must be in the building.

The red carpet has been rolled out for him. It sweeps up the marble steps and continues all the way to the furthest end of the landing. Inside, the theatre is spotless, opulent even, and Chester marvels once more at the contradiction between the building's somewhat grim facade and sumptuous interior. What did Geppetto make of this place when first he encountered it? He pictures the clown, travel-weary and bedraggled from his journey, and his heart lurches.

Chester tries both doors on the first level but is disappointed to find them locked. At the end of the landing, a narrow staircase winds upward to what he assumes must be the upper circle. The gods, with the cheapest seats and furthest from the stage. Overcome by the realization that he is intruding and could find himself in trouble, he is about to leave when he hears laughter.

Where is it coming from? He holds his breath and listens. It comes again, not from the landing but from the staircase. Either someone is in the upper circle or the sound is echoing from another part of the auditorium. The laughter has a hollow quality, distant. He is almost certain it is a woman's laugh.

Chester climbs the narrow stairs and finds the door to the upper circle unlocked. He enters an unlit space, with row upon row of tiered seating, and stands stock still. The stage is far in the distance and lit by a single spotlight. Chester can make out two people: a female artist, and a figure dressed in red. The laughter has stopped, and the artist has resumed painting. The figure sits on a stool in front of her, right leg crossed over left and elbow bent. In his hand he holds an object at a jaunty angle, as though displaying it, but Chester is unable to see what it is. He has a devilish look about him. Pointy grey beard, and a mask that covers the upper half of his face. On his feet are yellow slippers with pointed toes. Chester examines his memory, certain the figure stems from the *Commedia dell'Arte*. Indeed, it is none other than Pantalone, one of the principal characters who represents both ego and money.

What is fascinating is that although Chester is too far away to make out any detail, he is able to see that although the artist is evidently painting his portrait, the image appears abstract and fragmented with interlocking geometric shapes and vivid colours.

"Almost done." It is the artist who speaks, and Chester's heart flips. English, his native tongue. If he is not mistaken, he detected no hint of a foreign accent. Perhaps he can speak with her. If she is almost finished, does it mean she will leave soon? By the main door, perhaps? He cannot miss this opportunity. With fox-like stealth he slips out of the upper circle and hurries back down the stairs.

7

Feigning interest in the posters pasted on the foyer billboard, Chester waits. A minute or so later the door marked *Bancarelle* is flung open and in steps the actor dressed as Pantalone. He issues a wail of surprise on seeing Chester and a flourish of Italian ensues. Chester raises a hand in self-defence and flushes pink. "*Scusi.*" He points at the entrance. "It was open."

"Dis door shood be locked." He raises his mask and frowns.

"I was hoping—" Chester is so flustered that he has forgotten the line he prepared earlier. In fact, it does not seem an appropriate time to ask, since it is clear he should not be here. Instead, he touches the brim of his hat and heads for the door. About to push it open, he stops. "Actually..." He takes a breath. "*Conosci Geppetto?*"

The character dressed as Pantalone screws up his face. "Geppetto? De puppet maker?"

Chester swallows. "No, sir, a-a clown who goes by the name of Geppetto." The words sound ridiculous even to his own ears. All he has to go on is a fake name and a vague description of a tragic clown. What on earth is he doing? He notes the deep lines on Pantalone's forehead, the sagging jawline. Beneath the brim of his hat Chester's ears burn bright and a sweat breaks out on his forehead. "I'm sorry. Please...Allow me to start again."

The door to the stalls bursts open a second time. "Still here?" The artist stops in her tracks when she sees Chester, and she raises an eyebrow at Pantalone.

"Excuse me, Miss," Chester says. The artist, who wears a smear of red paint on her left cheek, narrows her eyes and Chester wonders if it is because of his presence or the fact that he refers to her as Miss. He glances at her ring finger, which is naked. "The door was open and... well, I'm looking for some-one. A man. A clown, actually, who goes by the name of Gep-petto. Apparently, he's been here in the past. He might even have worked here."

The actor dressed as Pantalone tuts in an exaggerated manner and waves an open hand. "I told him, we are not open." The artist ignores him and studies Chester's face, which makes him blush more deeply.

"Hmm," she says, biting the corner of her lip. "Geppetto, did you say?"

His stomach flips. *Does she know him?*

"Geppetto, the father of a fictional puppet brought to life in this very city?" Her smile is broad. "Yes, I think I've heard of him."

How foolish Chester feels. She is toying with him. In all likelihood she senses his discomfort and is intent on using it to her advantage. He shakes his head. "It doesn't matter." He touches his hat brim and nods, then pushes the door open.

"Wait!" She calls to him. "I am teasing. Please, forgive me."

Over a delicious lunch of ribollita and focaccia, Chester discovers that the artist, Eveline, has lived in Florence for just over a year, "…having come for the light," as she puts it, "and stayed for the food." She adores the theatre and, in return for complimentary tickets to performances and a little money, paints the portraits of opera singers and actors such as Arnaldo who plays Pantalone but who, in her words, is nothing like the fiend he plays and has a heart as soft as a pillow.

Her exuberance is contagious, and Chester gradually feels the knotted strings that are his thoughts loosen a little. Her candidness, along with the wine, grant him permission to admit that he has come in search of himself, as well as the clown named Geppetto. It is not good to divulge too much to strangers, he tells himself over and over, and yet with Eveline he feels compelled to do so.

Arnaldo on the other hand is more reserved. Stripped of his costume, his appearance is drab in comparison, and he looks older than Chester first imagined. Grey dress pants that have seen better days and a close-fitting black jacket that has worn to a shine at the elbows. Not a man of fortune, Chester thinks. The only item that marks him out as a man of the theatre is a jaunty crimson scarf, tied in a lopsided bow at the neck. His English is broken, but far in front of Chester's Italian. His gestures are the wildest thing about him.

"I 'av played at Pantalone more dan twenty years," he says, tweaking the corner of his moustache. "'Ere in Florence, but also in Paris. In fact, I would 'av been 'ere when your friend was 'ere, and I can tell you..." He pauses, and Chester holds his breath. "I never 'eard of 'im."

Chester deflates, and the conversation turns away from his search for Geppetto and moves to theatre and art, ending with Arnaldo inviting Chester to tonight's performance. "You must come," he says. "And Evie, too, zough she 'as seen it 'undred times."

Chester turns red and covers his nose with his fist. By and large, during lunch he has forgotten how much he detests what he considers to be his worst feature. However, the thought of sitting in the audience with a woman he has just met fills him with horror. Lunch with both of them is one thing, but without Arnaldo's company it would be something else. He does not have long to consider it before Eveline chimes in.

"My dear Arnaldo," she says. "Are you proposing a date?" Her laughter is the provocative kind, all teeth and sparkling eyes, without the slightest hint of embarrassment. Chester flushes deeper on her behalf.

"I-I wouldn't—" He doesn't know what to say. One half of him is already smitten; the other half horrified. So, instead, he raises a hand and rests his forehead on his palm.

"Shall we say eight-thirty then?" she says. "In the foyer?"

It is with little focus that Chester secures lodgings for the next few days and nights. His thoughts rest solely on Eveline, or Evie as Arnaldo calls her. Eveline...such a pretty name. It summons to mind the fae. Delicate, and yet delicate is not how he would describe her personality. Tall and slender, with a waist he is certain he could span, and yet there is a strength to Eveline that far outweighs his own.

He pictures her face as he shaves in the mirror. Her full lips, a slight cleft in the chin that adds to the sense of determination. But it is her eyes that make his heart lurch. Dark pools that slant a little at the inner corner. Eyes that take in all they see and keep it locked in a safe, secured behind a shiny keyhole in the shape of a pupil. A nick to the skin reminds him to focus on the task in hand. He dips the razor in the basin of water, watches the blood swirl in a foamy figure of eight.

Fumbling with the stud on his shirt collar, he wonders whether or not he should invite her to dinner after the performance. Would it seem too bold? On the other hand, it might seem rude not to. He rummages through his sparse luggage and pulls out the one tie and one scarf he has brought with him. The tie is dark maroon and a little frayed around the edges; the scarf, two shades of blue. A little livelier perhaps, though just as threadbare. He glances at the clock, wondering if he has time to go out and buy a new one, but decides the half an hour he has to spare will be better spent in calming himself. He does not wish to come across as a mumbling idiot, and right now he does not feel capable of making conversation.

At his age he should be far more at ease in women's company, married even, and yet in truth Chester has little experience with women. His troupe included many fine-looking girls, but he found them too flippant, too much surface and not enough depth. Not that he considers himself a catch, far from it, but were he to marry it would be to someone with whom he could share more than physical love. Someone with shared interests, or else he would grow bored over time, and the relationship would almost certainly fall apart. But what is he doing thinking about marriage? Today has been a chance encounter, nothing more, and tonight? Tonight will either be a disaster or it will lead to friendship. And yet he must admit, there's something special about Eveline. She frightens him a little, but at the same time he finds her interesting and alluring.

The *Commedia dell'Arte*. It takes fewer than five minutes for Chester to forget he sits next to Eveline, so enthralled is he by the performance. The tension drains from him like mercury from a thermometer, and his shoulders relax. Magnifico, the eagle-like leader of the city, a leader who looks down on all he surveys.

Punch, the pigeon-like peasant who has come to the city in search of work and who is all too ready to kiss the feet of his master.

And then there's Pantalone, the miserly merchant, played by Arnaldo. Chester is bewitched, in awe of his talent, and finds it difficult to reconcile the part he plays so seamlessly with the somewhat shambolic actor he had lunch with earlier.

Best of all though, is Harlequin, the acrobatic amoral servant who attempts to woo the enigmatic Columbina despite her father's disapproval. What Chester wouldn't give for just an ounce of Harlequin's guile. In Harlequin he recognizes similarities with his own performance as a tragic clown—the slapstick, the acrobatics—and yet there are also stark differences.

This performance tells a story. A story with magical elements and scenery changes that delight Chester and offer him hope. He has not laughed like this in a very long time, in fact the muscles in his cheeks ache from laughing. He steals a glance at Eveline and the warmth he feels increases a degree or two when he sees the joy on her face. She sees him watching and beams, then takes his hand in hers and squeezes it. And Chester's heart explodes.

During the interval, they eat the most delicious gelato Chester has ever tasted, and conversation flows so easily he forgets his troubles.

"As Arnaldo mentioned, I have seen the show several times now, but I never bore. Each time they perform they make it their own. I adore the improvisation and the way in which they create a story out of nowhere. It's rather like making art, don't you think?" Eveline wipes a trickle of gelato from Chester's chin with the tip of her finger and holds it in front of him, her smile broad and open.

"I'm sorry," he says, curling his toes inside his shoes. "How careless I am."

She looks at the mess on her finger. "What am I to do with it? I do not know you well enough to eat it, so I think you'd better do it."

Chester has no intention of licking the gelato off her finger. He plucks a handkerchief from his breast pocket, shakes it out, and hands it to her as fast as he can. He burns with embarrassment, though deep down he cannot help but admire her audacity. Why, the girls back home could be forthright, brash even, but Eveline doesn't so much as blink. It is as though social convention matters not one iota to her.

As if to prove the gesture is unimportant, she wipes her finger clean while talking at the same time, then passes the stained handkerchief back to him as though nothing has happened. "You know," she says, finishing her cone in two bites and licking her lips, "If you stay long enough, I could paint your portrait." She rests her chin on folded hands and studies his face, her dark eyes glinting with mischief.

Chester is lost for words. "I-I don't yet know how long I'll be staying. You see—"

She reaches across and turns his face to the side. "You have a strong profile. An artist's dream, though of course I would not necessarily paint you as you are." She frowns, and picturing how enormous his nose must look in profile, Chester tenses.

"Instead, I would paint you as I see you in my imagination." She tilts his head back to the centre, her fingers cool and gentle. Her eyes bore into his soul, and he cannot think of a single thing to say. The ring of the house-manager's bell announcing the end of the interval makes him start, but he is glad of the distraction. At this moment his feelings are so confused he does not know how to begin to analyse them.

He stands and offers her his hand, which she accepts graciously, then together they make their way back to their seats.

The curtains open and out peeps Harlequin against a forest backdrop, a mischievous grin on his face and footsteps nimble as mice.

"Do you know the history of the Harlequin?" Eveline whispers as Harlequin slips onto the stage.

Chester shakes his head.

"Remind me to tell you," she says, tapping the side of her nose.

If Chester considered the first act mesmerising then act two is even more so, for it introduces the audience to the character of Pierrot, a melancholic clown in whom Harlequin discovers a rival. The battle to court Columbina reminds Chester of his own situation, not in the way of plot but in the juxtaposition of character. Who will conquer? Harlequin with his upfront charm, or Pierrot with his unquestioning devotion? Chester fears it will be Harlequin, he whose surface charm outshines the more sincere. This is what life has taught him so far.

Performance over, Chester and Eveline leave the theatre together, her arm in the crook of his elbow.

"Hungry?" Chester asks. "We could have supper if you like."

She shakes her head and pats her stomach. "I'm still full from lunch." Her smile is genuine. "Another night, perhaps." Moonlight twinkles on the River Arno, turning her eyes to stars. "Now then, would you like to hear the story of Harlequin?"

His shoulders relax. "Indeed."

She squeezes his arm as they walk along the avenue and begins. "Harlequin, or Arlecchino as he is called in Italy, originated from the forest. A woodland creature of myth, a satyr of sorts. The lozenge-shaped patterns on his costume," she says, drawing a diamond in the air, "are in fact leaves."

Chester relaxes into her tale, the cool night air plucking wisps of hair free of her hat and making them dance so that she too appears to be a creature of the woods. A coat of deep green velvet and an orange tipped feather in her fashionable cloche enhances the effect.

"You have seen Cézanne's work on Harlequin, yes?" She stops outside an apartment block on Via Giotto.

"I-I'm not sure I have." Chester, assuming they have arrived at her home, is suddenly nervous in case she should invite him in.

"It's rather abstract," she says. "In the painting, Harlequin's face wears an impassive mask." She sweeps her fingers from forehead to chin, altering her expression from joy to austerity in one fell swoop, and he cannot help but wonder if the mask she wears is real.

Why does he find it so hard to trust? It is a fault in his genes, he is certain.

"I'd like to see it though. Is there a gallery we could visit? If you want to, that is." His boldness lights his face like a beacon, and he is glad of the darkness.

"Of course! This is Florence after all."

As Chester writes, his senses are awakened by the scents that waft from the five-hundred-year-old apothecary situated in the street below. Today, the sun is warm enough for Chester to open the window of his room in the lodging house. White muslin flutters in the breeze, resurrecting ghosts of the past who bring with them the bright green scent of geranium and a hint of warm peach, making his mouth water. He must remember to visit the apothecary before he leaves, perhaps he will purchase a gift for Eveline to thank her for making him feel welcome. If only he were bold enough.

He has arranged to meet her today, outside the Uffizi Gallery at three o'clock, and therefore must find a way to pass the time between now and then without falling apart.

Chester draws the scent of warm peaches deep into his lungs and picks up the pen.

Arlecchino (Harlequin)

by Runo Quill

I have no reason to dispute the story my mother told me the day I almost choked to death, and yet many of you will find it hard to believe.

A hot summer's day in the Tuscan hills, and mother and I were foraging. We stopped to rest and sample our wares on the trunk of a fallen cypress, when suddenly, having eaten a handful of wild blueberries, I found myself gasping for breath. She narrowed her eyes but did nothing to help.

"It's the peach stone," she said, her face as calm as a millpond. "I knew that one day this would happen."

While I turned red in the face, my mother ambled down to the river and returned with a measure of water, carried in the vessel she had been using to collect the blueberries. She passed it to me, and I gulped hard. The water tasted of moss and blueberry juice, but it soothed my throat and eased the choking sensation so that I was able to breathe.

A first breath. A re-birth.

She sat beside me and dried my tears with the hem of her skirts before spinning the tale of how I came to be. My origin story was about to unfold, and it was the strangest story I had ever heard.

"The old peach tree," she said. "The one in the far corner of Nonno's garden. Do you remember it?"

I shook my head and frowned, still shaken by my dice with death.

She sighed so deep I felt her deflate. Her arms hung limp, and her head bowed low.

"Your father," she said, but she did not look at me. "The peach tree."

"You make no sense, Mamma." I lowered myself from the tree trunk and lifted her chin so I could look into her eyes. In hers I saw my reflection, a boy on the brink of manhood. A boy encased in a body that felt both familiar and strange at the same time. My mother held out her forefinger and traced the bumpy protrusion on my throat with a delicate touch.

"Your father's seed," she said. "He planted it there one endless summer, long ago."

She turned her face away, leaned her back against the trunk, and closed her eyes. For several minutes she said nothing. Her breathing slowed, and I thought she had fallen asleep. I slumped down on the grass beside her and stroked the lump at the front of my throat with two fingers.

Never before had she mentioned my father, and whenever I asked, she would change the subject so that I learned not to ask. I thought on this now, as I lay in the warm grass, enveloped by the scent of rosemary.

"The tree." Her voice startled me from my daydream. "Your father," she said, "...the peach tree."

"What are you trying to say, Mother? Please, speak clearly."

She shook her head, and her eyes glistened with tears. "Impossible as it may sound, Arlecchino, the peach tree was your father. I-I have wanted to tell you this for such a long time but thought it best to wait until the evidence showed in your throat."

I pressed my fingers to the lump and swallowed, feeling the gristle move beneath the skin. Had my mother gone insane?

After what seemed like an age she said, "We loved each other deeply, the tree and I. Many summers I spent cradled in his arms, but he forbade me to taste his fruit until I turned sixteen." She flushed and ran her fingers along her collarbone, summoning the memory of his touch. Lost for words, I did not reply, and so she continued.

"His gnarled bark was strangely comforting, for it absorbed the sun and kept us both warm, even in winter." She had turned away from me, lost in the past. "Not too tall, your father. His strong arms, when laden with fruit, kissed the ground which made it easy for me to climb into his warm embrace." She shuddered, as though a breeze caressed her skin, and yet it hadn't. The day was still and ripe with gossip. Not so much as a blade of grass moved, such was its eagerness to hear the story. "And his peaches!" She licked her lips and turned to face me, and I recognized the girl she once was and felt nothing but love, despite the strangeness of her words.

"Ripe and full of juice, and sweet. Oh, so sweet! How could a girl resist?"

She patted the fallen tree trunk, inviting me to sit close to her, and I obliged.

"It's the reason you're always hungry, Arlecchino. How could you not be when something as delicious as he created you?"

It was true. My appetite had always been voracious, and yet despite this I did not grow fat. Quite the opposite in fact, for my limbs were as gangly as branches, my stomach taut and tanned. And now that I stood on the brink of manhood my hunger for other delicacies grew fierce, too, especially the maidens from the village and the near-naked naiads that frequented the water pool. I shifted my weight, uncomfortable about acknowledging such thoughts in my mother's presence. She noticed my discomfort and took my warm hand in her cool one to make me stay.

"You have my eyes, you know," she said, running a finger along the length of my brow. "My agility, too." She sprang from the tree trunk, deft as a nymph, and laughed. "You have his strength though. His strength and his fortitude." Her smile faded to sadness. "Come," she said, holding out a hand. "Something awaits you at home, something very precious that I have kept safe all these years."

We picked up our baskets and exchanged the fields and river for our home at the edge of the olive grove. As we walked, I begged her to reveal the secret of the forthcoming gift, but she declined, telling me to be patient or else she might change her mind and keep it hidden for one more year.

As instructed, I waited with bated breath in the tiny parlour while she disappeared into her bedroom.

Eventually she returned. "Close your eyes," she said, and I did as she asked. "Now hold out your hands."

The gift she gave me was substantial in weight, though cosseted in something smooth.

"Ready?"

I opened my eyes to see something wrapped in the softest sheath of the finest peach skin and covered in bright green leaves. An elongated shape beneath the wrapping, firm and slender.

Her chin quivered as she spoke. "When your father died, I stripped him bare, gathering every last leaf and fruit into my arms before removing the strongest of his limbs with a saw." She paused to calm herself then said, "Open it."

I unwrapped the sheath and discovered beneath its folds a wooden sword, engraved with the words *Il mio cuore, per sempre—My heart, forever*. The seed in my throat constricted, but I did my best to stem the flow. It was hard to believe that I held in my arms what was once part of my father. "It-it's exquisite." I smoothed the wood, tracing the curve of the grain, my father's blood, his life story, and found myself wondering in which year along the grain he met my mother.

She held out the wrapping, and I saw that the sheath I had discarded was a tunic, a tunic that would fit me to perfection.

"The peach skins I dried and stitched by hand," she said, inhaling the garment as she spoke. "For the leaves I needed a little help from the witch, Guibiana. It was she who taught me how to preserve the leaves so they would remain fresh and green for many years to come. See how they form a tessellating pattern?"

I nodded, but I must admit it was the sword that excited me most. Despite being hewn from wood, its tip was sharp as Eros's arrow, and I couldn't wait to try it out on some unsuspecting fool. The words she spoke next, though, brought me to my senses.

"Treasure it, Arlecchino." The scent of warm peach swirled about my head, its aroma manifesting in the form of a twisted branch. "May the skin of your father's fruit keep you warm, his leaves sustain you, his sword protect you. Most of all, may his love be with you, always."

So, my friends, you have learned my origin story. Many of you know me as the capricious swain of maidens, and this I cannot deny. Though dig beneath the skin and you will unveil flesh that is easily bruised by unrequited love.

8

Having re-read the story of Arlecchino, Chester realizes it is the most positive piece he has written to date. Yes, there is tragedy in the peach tree's demise, but the heart of the story is gentle and sweet. No hint of cynicism or regret; instead, the theme is one of love. When writing a story, he does not start out with the intention of writing something dark. It simply happens. So where has the light come from? Is it his new-found freedom in the land of olive groves and art, or is it meeting Eveline that has influenced him?

He edits the draft and reads it aloud. What if he were to make a copy and give it to Eveline? Chester has never shared his stories, except for one he had written as a child. The story had been about a black cat named Onyx and a mouse named Squeak. Hardly original, but then he had only been six years old. He had read it aloud at the dinner table, hoping to impress his family. Instead, he was laughed at, even though the story had a tragic ending.

"What's a boy your age doing writing stories?" his father had said. "Stories are for sissies. Now get outside and practise your stilt cycling. You've come a cropper a few times lately." His brother had sat with a spoon balanced on the tip of his nose, while his mother had pointed towards the door.

Eveline is different though. Florence is different. His stomach lurches at the thought of her reading the story, but his heart dares him nonetheless. He will see how their date at the museum goes before deciding, and besides, he will need to purchase some pretty notepaper first.

"So, what d'you think?" Eveline stops in front of the Cézanne and turns to Chester.

"Is this the painting you talked about? The portrait of Harlequin?"

"Of course. Who else?" Her eyes twinkle and he notices pretty dimples when she smiles. Chester finds it hard to turn his attention to the painting of a young Harlequin, garbed in a red and black suit, diamond patterned, with a ruffle at the neck.

"His expression," she says. "Happy or sad?" She hooks an arm in Chester's, and he tenses. He takes a deep breath, then permits his mind to accept the gesture. His arm relaxes in her grip, and he swallows.

"Not sure. If I'm honest, he looks bored."

"Hmm, and why do you say that?"

Chester studies the portrait, trying to interpret his response in a coherent sentence. One that won't make him sound like an idiot. He knows how these arty types can be—they have a knack of making themselves seem knowledgeable and others dull. Eveline's not like that though. That's the old Chester's cynicism taking a bite. "I don't really know. His stance, the way his head tilts to the side, his lack of grip on the sword."

Eveline smiles. "I agree. That's the impression I get too, but why do you think Cézanne chose to paint him like that?" Her arm is warm; her wrist narrow and elegant. Frail, but determined. He considers the question for quite some time, putting himself in the artist's shoes. Why, in his story about Harlequin, did he portray him as capricious? The same logic could be applied here, in interpreting Cézanne's intention.

"Perhaps he was bored when he painted it. I have no idea."

"And what if I tell you his son, Paul, posed for the painting? Would that change your mind?" Her lips twitch. The gallery is her domain, and she is relishing her dominion. It is enthusiasm that drives her, nothing else.

"Well, in that case, perhaps his son was bored."

Her face lights up. She squeezes his arm and moves on to the next painting—a female nude, small breasted, her hands folded in such a way as to barely cover the pubic area. Chester coughs into his free hand, uncomfortable with the thought of discussing a portrait of a naked woman with Eveline.

"Matisse," she says. "A favourite of mine."

He thinks about giving her a copy of the story, and the self-assurance he felt drains from him. She does not mince her words. If she thinks the story is rubbish, then she will say so.

"Thoughts?" she says, nudging him in the rib.

"Well, I'd like to know why he calls it *Study in Blue* for one thing. He is manoeuvring the focus towards the artist's use of colour rather than the subject, to deflect his embarrassment."

Eveline senses his discomfort and comes to his aid. She raises an eyebrow. "What about her face, Chester? How do you imagine she's feeling?"

He takes a breath.

"It's not a trick question, you know. You must remember that in art there is no right and wrong answer." A squeeze of the arm. "That is what I love about it."

He relaxes somewhat. "It's difficult to tell because the face lacks detail."

She tilts her head, waiting.

"If I had to guess, I'd say coy. A little embarrassed perhaps. Maybe modelling is new to her." He points towards the face and scratches his chin. "See, the complexion is redder than the rest of her body...and the chin. It points downwards."

"You see, Chester. There is much to glean from so little detail."

Chester considers her words, thinking about his own work. The way in which he likes to leave certain aspects open to interpretation. Perhaps she will enjoy his story. He opens his mouth to speak, but the words will not come.

"Are you all right?" she asks, "You seemed about to say something."

"It's nothing."

"Come now, Chester. Don't be shy. Was it something about the painting?"

A shake of the head. "No, no—actually, it made me think about something else. Your words, I mean."

"Which words?"

"What you said about there being much to glean from so little detail."

"And?"

He sighs and shuffles his feet. "All right, I'll tell you. As long as you promise not to laugh."

"Don't be silly." She smiles, and his throat constricts. "It's just that—well, I write stories. Stories that no one ever gets to read because I cannot bring myself to share them in case—"

Her grip on his arm is a vice. "Oh, how wonderful! Do you have one with you?"

Her enthusiasm both excites and terrifies him. "Of course not, but-but I can bring one for you next time. If you want, that is."

She releases his arm, claps her hands, and gives a squeal of excitement, causing several people in the gallery to frown and tut, which fails to perturb her in the slightest. "Please do! When can I see it?"

"Arnaldo's arranged for me to meet with the theatre manager tomorrow afternoon, so perhaps I could give it to you then. After the meeting, I mean...or before if that suits you better." Realizing he sounds desperate, Chester stops speaking and waits for her to respond.

"Shall we have dinner? I know of a nice little restaurant on the banks of the Arno. They serve the best panna cotta, drizzled in maraschinos." She licks her lips. "Mmm! Sweet and sharp at the same time."

Her suggestion thrills him, but still he holds back. "If you're sure. I feel as though I've commandeered enough of your time these past few days. In fact, I feel rather guilty."

"Don't be silly. Oh, and don't forget to bring the story with you."

Arnaldo awaits Chester's arrival on the steps of the Teatro Verdi and greets him with an air kiss to both cheeks, which makes Chester flush red. "*Ciao*, Chester! Eez good to see you. Come in, come in." Arnaldo is half-dressed for tonight's performance—yellow slippers, red costume, but no mask or make-up as of yet.

In the inside pocket of Chester's jacket is Geppetto's journal. He pats his pocket protectively, just as he has done every few minutes since placing it there.

"Matteo is-a waiting in de of-fice. E said to bring you dere." He hooks his arm in Chester's, much as Eveline had done, and marches him up the steps and into the foyer. Arnaldo speaks incessantly as he weaves a path through the theatre, but Chester's thoughts are elsewhere. He is remembering the last time he went to see Duke, the troupe master back home. The time he had confided in him about feeling out of sorts and in need of a change. What a disaster that had been. But this is different, he tells himself. He has not come to ask about work, he has come to ask if he remembers someone by the name of Geppetto, and if not, then someone who might fit the description of such a person.

Within moments, they arrive at a door marked *Ufficio*, and Arnaldo barges in without knocking. "Matteo—Chester;

Chester—Matteo," he says with a flourish. His grin is wide, and Chester notices for the first time that one of his lower teeth is made of gold. It winks in the light cast by the lamp on Matteo's desk, making him appear rather roguish.

"Ah, Chester. Good to meet you. Please, sit down," Matteo says.

"Good to meet you, too." Chester pats his jacket pocket, then sits.

"I'll leave you to it," Arnaldo says, taking a small bow.

Matteo has the look of an Italian, but his English is impeccable. Hardly a hint of accent when he speaks. He must have lived in England at some point, Chester assumes, and he is right because the next thing Matteo says is, "Where are you from exactly? London? I spent my formative years there, brought up by my paternal grandparents after my mother passed away."

"London, yes." Chester slips Geppetto's journal from his inside pocket and opens it to the first page.

Matteo lights a fat cigar, offers Chester the same, which he declines, then leans back in his chair.

"This might sound rather strange," Chester says, "but a little while ago I came across this journal quite by chance, and it—well, let's say it struck a chord." He leans across the desk and points to Geppetto's name and then to the lines that speak of Geppetto's time at the Teatro Verdi.

Matteo frowns and puffs at the cigar, sending curls of smoke in Chester's direction. Chester stymies a cough, then closes the book. He doesn't want it tarnished by smoke.

"And?" Matteo circles a stout finger in the air.

"And I hoped you might remember him."

"And why, may I ask, is it imperative you find him?"

Chester curls his toes inside his oversized shoes. "It's difficult to explain. I felt a connection, I suppose, and—and he encouraged me to follow in his footsteps."

Matteo guffaws, which brings on a bout of coughing. Once he has composed himself, he says, "I can tell you now, the only Geppetto I know of is the one in the story of the wooden puppet. Pinocchio, or whatever he was called." He points at the journal which now rests in Chester's lap. "If whoever wrote that is suggesting he once worked here, he's either lying, or he's used a…what d'ya call it?" He whirls the finger again, close to his right ear. "Pseudonym." He bangs the desk, leaving behind a puddle of ash. "That's the word I'm looking for!"

Chester is sorely disappointed. His face falls and his shoulders sag in defeat.

Matteo takes another puff of cigar before replacing it in the ashtray from where it points at Chester like an accusatory finger. "Cheer up, son," he says. "Just because I don't recognize the name, it doesn't mean he wasn't here. Tell you what, give me some dates and a bit more information and I'll look through the staffing records."

Chester opens his mouth to speak, then closes it again. How can he explain that he has no dates? Matteo will think him mad. He squirms in his seat, thinking how idiotic he has been in coming here expecting to find answers. Matteo is waiting. He has to give him something. "I'm afraid I have no definitive dates, only supposition." He takes a deep breath and swallows. "The man I speak of seemed knowledgeable about this theatre and the *Commedia dell'Arte* in particular. His journal gives me no reason to suspect him of fraud." He winces at the words, despite them being true. "Do you think you might look at the records? Just to see if something sparks a memory?"

Matteo heaves a sigh. "My dear boy, you have no idea how transient actors are here. They come and go like the plague." He shakes his head and picks up the cigar which has all but died out. "I'm afraid if you can't give me a date, it'll be a pointless exercise." He rises from the chair and holds out a hand for Chester to shake. Seeing his disappointment he says, "Tell you what I will do. I'll ask around, especially the staff who have been here some time, to see if anyone fits the bill." He raises an eyebrow. "I'll let Arnaldo know if anything surfaces, okay?"

It is with a heavy heart that Chester returns to the lodging house. The outcome of the meeting with Matteo has been disappointing to say the least. Why is tracking Geppetto proving to be so elusive? The journal inside his jacket is a leviathan. Geppetto's words are laden with dark ink and deception. Where will he go from here? To another form of lodging in the city or somewhere entirely different? One thing he knows for certain is that he can't go home. Not now, not ever. He knows he can't survive on his savings for long and will need to find work, be it in the theatre or something different altogether. *You lack ambition, Chester. That's your problem. Ambition and stickability.* It's his father's voice he hears, and the words rile him. Ambition means one thing only as far as his father is concerned, and that is to rise among the ranks within the troupe. When his father speaks of stickability he refers to the close-knit realms of their social circle. Woe betide anyone who might wish to see something of the world, and woe betide anyone who desires to break away.

How must his family be feeling right now? he wonders. Angry? Upset? Or will they have already denounced him a usurper and moved on?

Back in his room, and with three hours to spare before meeting Eveline, he replaces the journal in his dressing table drawer and swaps it for the story of Arlecchino which he has copied out to give to her, then allows himself to drift.

Chester arrives at the Trattoria del Fagioli restaurant half an hour before he is due to meet Eveline. Should he order a drink and wait, or take a walk along the banks of the river? He decides on the latter, since it is a glorious evening. The excitement he felt at the port of Dover seems aeons away. The sense of adventure, of having escaped a life of imprisonment feels like a dream.

A chevron of wild geese swoops low above the river, in battle formation. Chester pauses his step to watch them land. Splayed feet, wide-winged, white forms tinged pink by the setting sun. A moment of graceful beauty, and not a concern in the world. He wishes the moment had been shared with Eveline, and the thought of seeing her again lifts his spirits. He pats the pocket of his jacket, which contains the story of Arlecchino.

In Eveline, he has met someone like no other, someone who dreams big and shrugs off the trappings of polite society. She is her own woman, and he must be his own man. Instead of dwelling on disappointment, he must make his own decisions instead of being led by some fictional puppet master. The geese issue a honk of approval, and Chester translates their voice as meaning, *Do not allow yourself to be sent on a wild goose chase.* He mutters his appreciation, then turns around and walks back along the banks of the Arno in the direction of the restaurant.

Chester's heart flutters as Eveline approaches from the opposite direction. She waves and quickens her step, while he stops and turns red.

"Chester," she says, her arms wide open. "You look a little flummoxed. Are you okay?"

He does not walk into her embrace, he simply cannot. How is it possible that she looks even more beautiful than the previous day? Her complexion glows in the evening sun, and her eyes twinkle as though she sees deep inside his soul. He takes her hand and plants the lightest of kisses on her cheek, though it pains him to do so. Not because he doesn't want to. He would love to embrace her fully. It's just that he hasn't come far enough to grant himself the permission he needs to open himself to another person, especially one as vivacious and warm as Eveline.

"How did the meeting go?" she asks as they enter the restaurant.

"Not good," he says. "The manager has never heard of Geppetto." He shrugs. "A fool's errand, I suppose."

"Don't say that, Chester. I for one am glad you came to Florence."

The waiter interrupts before he has chance to reply. "Signore, Signora, this way please." He guides them towards a window table from where they will be able to watch the sun set over the river. As they take their seats, Chester experiences a sensation of exponential bliss, one that makes all negative thoughts dissipate into thin air. He beams at Eveline. "And I am very glad to have met you too."

They turn their attention to the menu, Eveline enthusing over dishes she has previously tasted and encouraging Chester to be bold in his choice of main course. "Now then," she says once they have placed their order. She holds out a hand. "The story, if you please."

Chester places a protective hand over his jacket pocket. "Oh no," he says, panic rising to his throat. "I remembered to bring it." He teases the corner of the envelope out of the pocket then pushes it back in. "But you shall have it when we bid each other goodnight. Not a moment before. I-I couldn't bear to sit and watch you read it."

Eveline pouts and tilts her head to the side. "Oh, Chester," she says, breaking into a smile. "You're such a tease."

The evening is a success. Chester cannot recall a time when he felt so at ease in another person's company. With Eveline, he almost forgets about his huge nose and feet the size of barges. They talk about art and literature, and Chester tells her how he would visit the Reading Rooms in Magician's Quarter, a forbidden place, where temptation lurked in the form of en-lightenment and knowledge of faiths and religions other than his own. As he speaks, the words reinforce the sense that the Clown God Cholly, is nothing more than a distant echo. A thing of the past. His fictitious image a tool to elicit fear and control. He closes his eyes and pictures the huge round face of the clown god—the insincere grin that splits it from ear to ear. An inordinate number of teeth, yellowed and rotten.

Red-rimmed irises that bore into the soul of whoever looks upon it. He shivers.

"You cold, Chester?" Eveline's voice summons him back to the present.

He shakes his head. "No, no. It's just that I was somewhere else for a moment, that's all." He refuses to tell her where though, even when she pinches the skin on the back of his hand and pleads. He cannot talk about Father Roly and the Sacred Church of Razzmatazz, and he will not speak of the Clown God Cholly. How long does it take to rid oneself of one's past? he wonders. How far does one need to venture before the burden is eradicated for good?

Arm in arm, they make their way home. Has there ever been a more romantic evening? Chester wonders. The stars twinkle. The moon is a shimmering silver scarf on the surface of the river, and Chester breathes in hints of jasmine and the warm scent of algae.

"I must leave Florence soon," he says as they stop outside her apartment. He clears his throat, considering his words. By now he had expected Geppetto to have made himself known. Either that or to have provided further information on where Chester should go next. He cannot sit around waiting, living a life of luxury forever.

She pouts. "So soon? But where will you go?"

"I really cannot say. Coming here has been..." How has it been? In many ways heartening, but in one way disappointing. He squeezes her hand, and in a rare moment of bravery he lifts her chin and kisses her lightly on the lips. "I-I'm sorry. I shouldn't have—"

Her smile lights up her face. "No need to apologize, Chester." She fixes him with her gaze, and before he has chance to think about it, he kisses her again, this time more passionately.

"Will we keep in touch?" she asks, once he releases her.

"Of course," he says. "I'd love to." He hands her the envelope containing the story of Arlecchino, and his bravery drains from him. "I hope you enjoy it, but if not, it doesn't matter."

She strokes the paper, tracing her name on the front. "Chester, you underestimate yourself. Please write once you settle in your new place. I'll be sad to see you leave."

"I will, I promise. And thank you for showing me around Florence and for—for everything." He pulls her close and kisses her cheek, then walks away with his heart in his mouth.

The night air chills as a breeze whips up out of nowhere. Chester pulls up his jacket collar and plunges his hands deep in his pockets. The streets are all but deserted now, this part of Florence being away from the main strip and far less fashionable.

It is as he rounds the corner of the street in which his lodgings are situated that he sees him. A tall gentleman dressed head to toe in black. The man stands outside the lodging house, tweaking his moustache and smoking, but the moment he sees Chester he hurries down the street with his head bowed low. There's something familiar about him, though Chester cannot place it. He stops in his stride and watches as the man approaches the street corner. As he does so, the streetlamp catches the man's coat pocket, highlighting something white. Not a handkerchief—more like a card of some kind. The magician! The magician from the Reading Rooms. Chester is certain they are one and the same, but how can they be? Then, like a gust of wind, the man dressed in black disappears.

Chester shakes his head. Coincidence, surely? His thoughts about the magician are subverted by the sudden realization that Eveline is likely to be reading the story of Arlecchino at this precise moment. He pictures her curled on the sofa, laughing as she reads, or shaking her head in disapproval. Eveline is not cruel, he tells himself, but he is not easily persuaded. Forgetting all about the man dressed in black, he hurries up the stairs to his room, the need to re-read and judge the story for himself overwhelming.

He opens the drawer of his dressing table and pulls out his notebook before throwing off his jacket and sprawling on the bed. *Arlecchino, by Runo Quill.* The romance between Arlecchino's mother and father seems inept on this reading. Ridiculous even. How could a woman fall in love with a tree? And yet he cannot help but feel that the love between Arlecchino's parents is similar to his feelings for Eveline—illogical, the stuff of dreams. As an artist, he hopes she will be able to see beyond the surreality.

Exhausted now, Chester cannot think straight. It is not the best time for making judgements, but tomorrow he will need to decide what his next step must be.

It is as he replaces the notebook in the drawer that he sees it—Geppetto's journal is missing. Certain he replaced it after meeting with Matteo, he swipes his hand from one side of the drawer to the other, then yanks the drawer from the cabinet, hoping the journal has fallen down the back. All to no avail. The journal is missing. A surge of alarm, as the man dressed in black looms large in his vision. Has he stolen it from Chester's room? If he fails to find it, he will wake the landlady. She needs to know if someone has entered the building without permission.

He pictures himself returning from the meeting. He had swapped the journal for the copy of the story, he is certain. His heart pounds as he searches the room. What few possessions he has are thrown from their resting place until the room resembles a crime scene. Tension builds, and despite it being close to midnight he pays no heed to the slumber of other guests. Although the journal has proven pointless, he feels an attachment to it. One he cannot relinquish. In a last-ditch attempt, he throws the coverlet off the bed, and there, tucked between sheet and blanket, lies the journal.

Relief courses through his veins. Cross-legged on the bed, he thumbs through the book to the last entry.

> *Our journey has come to an abrupt end, or so it would seem. Trust me when I say that it has not. In fact, it is just beginning. The answers you seek await you in Florence, at the Teatro Verdi, home of the Commedia dell'Arte!*
>
> *Come, be my honoured guest!*

What answers? He has found none. He flicks through the remaining pages, expecting to find them blank, but he is mistaken. The clown known as Geppetto has been in his room and has written a new chapter. So surprised is he to see the words on the paper that he cannot decide which to do first—read them or wake the landlady and admonish her for allowing a stranger to enter his room. Are Geppetto and the magician one and the same? It is possible. The thought of someone rifling through his belongings unnerves him.

He checks his wallet and travel documents, relieved to discover neither is missing.

Propping himself up on the pillows, he reads the second entry in Geppetto's journal.

> *If my lack of presence thus far has disappointed you, then I ask for your forgiveness. I wanted you to see for yourself how engaging life outside of the microscopic world in which you live can be, and that takes time. Trust me, it was for your own good that I waited before showing my hand.*

Showing his hand? Could the phrase be an errant slip of the pen on the magician's part?

> *So, mission accomplished, I am ready to tell you about the next stage of my journey and implore you to follow me. But before we leave Florence, I must speak of how deeply my time spent at the Commedia dell'Arte moved me and hope you felt something of the same. Not only were the performances riveting, but they made me appreciate the artistry within the profession of clowning. Like you, I had been forced to limit my experience to our own small circle. Taught not to widen my horizons and learn about other forms of our art, but seeing how innovative, how free flowing the work of the actors could be made me reconsider abandoning the profession altogether. First, I believed I should educate myself in its various forms before deciding on my future.*

What a character Harlequin is! I admired his guile and wit so much that I would have given anything to have swapped places with him. My admiration for Harlequin led me to discover Pierrot. A melancholic figure, one whose roots lie in stock comedy and pantomime, but Pierrot is far more complex than that. His unrequited love for Columbine (since she preferred Harlequin) fails to realize the depth of his personality.

Geppetto's journal describes at length the merits of Pierrot. It is apparent that Geppetto holds him in high regard, to the point of hero worship, almost. Of course, Chester has read about Pierrot, but he has not had the good fortune to see a live performance. Fascinated by the way in which Pierrot has transformed from a stock comedic character to one with so much depth throughout the centuries is of great interest. The subversion of language, the use of mime, has elevated Pierrot to become a muse for artists and writers. From poets to playwrights, painters to musicians, Pierrot has captured the attention of those who want to understand the alienated fellow-sufferer and express it through art.

Why, even Pierrot's appearance has metamorphosed over time, from the stock white-faced, white-suited performer to something boundless in spirit and androgynous in nature.

So follow me to Paris, the city you paused at en-route to Florence, and discover for yourself the astounding talent of Pierrot, for it is in Paris that the melancholic clown first morphed from his Italian counterpart, Pedrolino.

According to Geppetto's journal, Pierrot is isolated, seemingly out of touch with the rest of society. A solitary voice who bears the pathos of the artists who have painted him, artists such as Watteau, Gill and Gérôme.

Chester thinks of Eveline, and wonders if she knows of the paintings. He must remember to ask when he writes. It will make a good icebreaker, especially as separation often leads to a cooling of the heart. Will he feel this too, or will his passion for her continue to burn? The latter, he imagines, if the ache inside him whenever he pictures her is anything to go by.

Geppetto ends with the words:

> *Pack up your bags and your sorrows and prepare yourself for the majesty that awaits you at the Théâtre Déjazet!*
> *I look forward to seeing you there.*

Despite the lateness of the hour, Chester is fully alert. He does as Geppetto suggests and packs, so that he can leave first thing in the morning. He won't even bother to question the landlady about the intruder. He is certain she will know nothing, so what is the point of causing ill feeling when he is about to leave?

9

Chester arrives in Paris as the sun is about to dip below the horizon. It bruises the sky and turns La Seine to blood. Exhausted by the day's travel, he seeks the first form of lodging he can find—a basic *chambre d'hôte*, situated next to a patisserie on the Rue de Poitou.

"*Combien de nuits?*" the proprietor asks, giving Chester the once-over from behind little round glasses that remind him of Toulouse-Lautrec.

Chester shuffles his feet, unsure of how long he should book for. "Just one night, please. I'll let you know tomorrow if I intend to stay longer."

The proprietor frowns, and Chester wonders whether it's because his English is poor or because he is booking a single night.

"*Une nuit?*"

"*Oui.*"

He thrusts a registration book at Chester and points. "Name," he whirls a finger in the air, "etcetera."

Chester considers asking how far away the Théâtre Déjazet is but thinks better of it. "*Merci.*" He pauses, attempting to locate the French word for breakfast, but fails. "Breakfast?"

The proprietor shakes his head. "*Non.*" He points towards the door. "*Patisserie, ou café.*" He holds up his hands as if he is not to blame, then gives Chester a room key. "*Chambre trois,*" he says, pointing to the stairs.

The room, as Chester suspected, is clean but sparsely furnished, with a single metal bed frame, thin mattress, and a hanging space for his clothes. No desk or table, not even a bedside cabinet. Unsuitable for writing anything more than a postcard. Even that will have to wait, as when he writes to Eveline he wants to provide a more permanent address. He will leave here in the morning, so there is little point in unpacking anything other than his wash-kit.

In the tiny bathroom down the hall, he examines his face in the mirror before shaving. It must be a trick of the light because his nose looks a little less bulbous. He turns sideways and examines his profile, probing and flattening his nose with two fingers. He looks down at his feet and wiggles his toes, then rubs a hand over his abdomen, feeling his ribcage. He has lost weight over the last few weeks, so much so that he can count three ribs on each side. Why, even his shoes feel a little loose.

Ablution complete, he returns to his room, hungry but too tired to go out into the city. He will make do with the apple and bag of walnuts that lurk at the bottom of his bag.

The following morning, as soon as the sun has risen, he pays his bill, then purchases a croissant and coffee from the patisserie next door. A squared *jardin* is close by, so he finds an empty bench and shares his breakfast with the pigeons before purchasing a map of the city and a guidebook from a nearby kiosk.

Théâtre Déjazet is situated a half mile north, on the Boulevard du Temple. Chester ponders over whether he should make his way there first or look for more permanent lodgings, somewhere he can stay for a few weeks at least. He has enough money to cover him for a month or two, by which time he will either need to find work or return home.

Take your time, Geppetto's journal had suggested. *Paris is a spectacular city, and you should explore it fully.* How much time though? A week? A month? A year?

That Chester still has faith in the former clown is questionable, but what does it matter? He has escaped the drudgery of the life he knew and is intent on making a new life.

Chester heads in the direction of the Théâtre Déjazet, taking in his surroundings. Over the last week he has altered his stride, and this pleases him. The splayed feet have all but disappeared, and he has rid himself of the impulse to spin cartwheels or leap from bollards. Shaking off old habits feels good, yet when he considers the fact that he no longer stands out from the crowd he feels a little irked. Is this normality? Blending in with the crowd to the point of becoming invisible? And if so, is that what he wants? His thoughts give rise to panic, which in turn makes him breathless, so he stops in front of the Place de la République and rests on the steps beneath the bronze statue of Marianne, Goddess of Liberty.

Once calm, he dips into the guidebook, considering where to go after the theatre.

Théâtre Déjazet nestles among cafes and several other theatres of similar size on the Boulevard du Crime, so called, according to Chester's guidebook, because of the large number of crimes that have been committed on stage here. Set back from the wide road and accessible via a flight of steps, the theatre boasts posters of clown performances, including portraits of Pierrot, as well as a comedy drama *Les Femmes Collantes*. A matinee performance featuring Pierrot begins at two o'clock. Chester checks his pocket watch and finds he has more than four hours to spare, ample time to find lodgings. But where to start? It is one thing to find a hotel for the night, but quite another to find somewhere more permanent.

He continues along the Boulevard, wondering what to do next, when his attention is drawn to a poster in the window of a tabac. *Montmartre*, it says in blazing red letters, *maison de l'avant-garde!* The poster depicts a buxom woman, dressed in red and black, standing in front of a row of buildings with jagged rooftops and tall chimneys. The name Montmartre is familiar. Of course, he had mentioned it in *The Three Lives of Quasimodo*. He scratches the depths of his memory, searching for other snippets of information. Toulouse-Lautrec, the infamous painter, known for his depiction of the Parisian underground. His guidebook informs him that Montmartre is some three miles north, in the eighteenth district. *A bizarre realm, swarming with artists, writers and musicians of every denomination, from circus to the sultry,* according to the guidebook. Chester's heart soars. Could there be a more tempting advertisement? His thoughts turn to Eveline, wishing she were here with him. For some moments, he allows his mind to wander a path where the two of them share a life, before turning his attention back to the book.

Montmartre is perched atop a hill, or *butte* as it is called. *The higher you climb the butte, the more affordable the rents*, the guidebook says. On the opposite side of the road a tram awaits, destination unknown.

Chester crosses to the other side and leans into the tram. "Montmartre?" he asks.

"*Oui,*" the driver says. "*Dix minutes.*"

Chester alights the tram at the lower tier of the *butte*. Late morning, and the district is still asleep. As an area renowned for its nightlife, Chester is unsurprised. Drawn shutters, closed blinds, only the occasional cafe or street vendor is awake. A Burmese cat sprawls in the sunny doorstep of a fishmonger, hoping for a treat of some kind once the vendor awakens. When it sees Chester it rises and purrs, rubbing against his trouser leg. He picks it up and strokes the base of its ears, a swell of emotion in his throat as he thinks of Arlo. Reluctantly, he puts the cat down, refusing to turn back around. Now is not the time to get smitten by a cat.

As the district awakens, so do Chester's senses. Sweet pastries from the patisserie, freshly baked bread. Such shops lie side by side with glitzy cafes and concert halls. A colourful and enticing array of posters advertise the wares of theatres and dance halls, and Chester finds the urge to stop and savour them irresistible.

The croissant he shared with the pigeons earlier did little to satisfy him, but now that he is here his hunger resumes. He sits outside a cafe, armed with coffee, a warm baguette, and Camembert, and drinks in the atmosphere. This part of the city feels more tangible somehow, more alive. With its emphasis on entertainment, it reminds him of Clown Quarter, only here it feels more authentic.

A thought occurs to him, one he believes he should have considered much earlier. Turin, Florence, and now Paris. All three cities are divided into districts or quarters, just like London, and while it is true to say that each quarter has its own flavour, the lines between them are far less distinct than those back home, blurred around the edges. He closes his eyes and pictures the luridness of Clown Quarter. The brightly coloured Church of Razzmatazz and the rainbow-coloured apparatus in the schoolyard. He takes a mental journey along the streets until he reaches the crossroads where Clown Quarter and Magician's Quarter intercept. Are the lines really as distinct as he imagines? He conjures a memory. A pavement cafe, just off the intersection. A whitefaced clown, vaguely familiar though not from his alley. He plays at poker with a magician dressed in black, the two of them locking eyes before making their next move. But as Chester watches, the ruffle at the clown's neck morphs into an elaborate bow tie. Bowler becomes top hat, the clown's menacing grin twists into a handlebar moustache until he no longer sees a clown and a magician but two of the same.

He drains his coffee, and before he can replace the cup on the saucer the waiter appears and asks if he requires anything else. The waiter's English is good, so Chester takes the opportunity to ask about lodgings.

The waiter smiles and casts his eyes over Chester's clothes. "Depends. A small apartment higher up is okay, but here, in the heart of the arrondissement, rents are bigger." He balances the dishes in one expert hand and points north with the other.

"Only the rich and famous live here, which is why I live at the top." He shrugs and smiles.

"And how might I find somewhere?" Chester says. "Is there a newspaper?"

"Newspaper, yes, but unless you speak fluent French, is hard. But many English and Americans living here, so is not so bad. Look for the postcards in newsagents and also...how you say... *L'agent immobilier*?" He scratches his head with his free hand.

"Estate agent?" Chester says.

"Ah, *oui*, estate agent. Is one along road."

Chester looks in the direction in which the waiter points. "And work?" he says. "How might I find work?"

"Work? What is it you do?"

Chester opens his mouth to speak, then pauses. What does he do? If he is no longer a clown, then what is he? His stomach sinks, but his curiosity rises. Does the waiter not recognize the clown in him? He swallows hard. "The theatre," he says, "but I am hoping for a change."

"You are in right place for theatre. Much work here. But change?" He shakes his head. "Not so much, unless you want to wait at table like me."

"I see," Chester says, handing him a tip. "*Merci*. Thank you for your time."

Chester heads in the direction of the estate agent, considering his most recent interactions. The waiter, the proprietor at the hotel. Neither guessed his background, or if they did they were too polite to say so. There is no shame in being a clown, so why would they be reluctant to mention the fact that they recognized the clown in him? He rubs his nose and looks down at his feet. Yes, he still bears the marks of the trade. How could he not?

Chester leaves the estate agents with two hours to spare before the matinee and three small apartments to view the following day, all of which are close to the top of the *butte*. Cheered by the morning's events he heads south to find lodging for the night before returning to the Théâtre Déjazet for the afternoon performance. Of course he could go another day, but he is eager to see what Geppetto saw. If the right moment occurs, he might ask after Geppetto, but if it doesn't, then he'll wait until the former clown decides to announce himself.

Leaving behind the bright sunshine of the city, Chester blinks repeatedly as he enters the relative dark of the auditorium. He stumbles down the aisle, keen to choose a seat as close to the stage as possible. Third row, centre position, he folds his jacket and rests it on his lap, then waits for the performance to start. A melancholy tune from the orchestra pit, the low-pitched cello, the slow tempo of the violin, the stage is in total darkness. The audience falls to a hush, and Chester is able to detach himself from the outside world.

A spotlight, centre-stage. Pierrot sits on a stool, shoulders hunched and expression vacant. The white-faced clown gazes out toward the audience. Pale as the moon and silent as the grave, what follows is an act of such heartsick, torturous sadness that Chester is transported from his seat, straight into the mind of the figure on stage. Pierrot's grace and poise, his existential suffering laid bare to those in tune with his character.

In Pierrot he recognizes the internal anguish of one who is an island. His white face is a crystal mirror, his tears black diamonds from the bowels of the earth. Only when his own tears salt his lips does Chester realize he is crying. In this theatre, in this one act, his fate is sealed.

Chester must cut the umbilical cord of the clown for good. He cannot return to London, even if it means starving to death.

10

By the time Chester reaches the foot of the *butte,* the sun has risen to its peak. No tram today, since his first appointment with the estate agent isn't until one o'clock, he has walked all the way from the third district in an attempt to shed the melancholy that devoured him during yesterday's theatre performance. Thus far, he has failed to do so.

The cobbled, winding streets of Montmartre are a whirl of colour. Jugglers and buskers, portrait painters and puppeteers, each with their own distinctive style. Shops and street vendors selling everything from cheap souvenirs to sweet roast chestnuts. An assault on the senses. The hustle and bustle dampen the heat of his mood and nibbles a corner off his sorrow. *Life is an adventure*, he tells himself time and time again, but the sentiment is too frail to make its mark.

Montmartre is riddled with theatres and galleries. Each and every street a glutton of entertainment. Clown Quarter back home has nothing on this, despite its garish appearance. And yet Chester cannot help but feel swamped by all the noise and colour. Today, it feels overbearing.

The higher he climbs, the calmer the streets grow, until he finds himself on the Rue Saint-Vincente where he is due to meet the agent. His pocket-watch informs him he has arrived fifteen minutes early, so he walks the length of the street in search of the apartment and finds it situated at the far end, next to a small boutique selling everything from hats to handkerchiefs. After the bustle of the strip, he is glad of the relative calm, even if the buildings look rather unkempt.

Paramount in his thoughts is the fact that he only has sufficient funds to last a few weeks, so since this is the most affordable of the three properties, he hopes it will suffice, at least for the time being, until he finds work. In watching Pierrot's performance he has done what he came here to do, but it has left a greater void in him than ever. A gaping wound that refuses to heal. He pictures himself on the journey home, humiliated and defeated. *Ready to eat humble pie?* his mother would chide. No sympathy for his plight, no understanding. He would rather it all end than give her the pleasure.

The tiny apartment consists of one room, but at least it has a table overlooking a backdrop of greenery. The smell of fried onion drifts across the stairway from the shared kitchen, but it is relatively clean and currently free of tenants. A bathroom at the end of the first landing consists of a toilet, hand basin, and a child-sized slipper bath, tarnished with soap scum.

"I'll take it," he says, pulling out his wallet and counting out notes.

"But you have not seen the others," the estate agent says. "You might prefer—"

Chester hands over enough francs to cover the deposit, plus the first week's rent. "It's fine, at least I have a view."

Within the space of an hour, Chester has secured a place to stay and is winding his way back down the *butte* in search of work, determined to take anything he can find, even if it means waiting at tables. He stops outside a corner shop and browses the postcards that hang on a wire frame. Eager to write to Eveline, he chooses one depicting a quaint little cafe, complete with striped awning, and leans against the shop window to write it. She will forgive the wobble in his handwriting, he is certain.

His words, though brief, paint a colourful picture of Montmartre and a monochrome view of his apartment. He does not mention the story of Arlecchino, though he hopes her reply might do so.

Now, where to find work? He has been idle long enough. If he fails to find work in Montmartre, then he will need to widen his search.

Having purchased a copy of *Le Petit Parisien* from a street vendor, he orders a light lunch at a street cafe and opens the paper to the *Offres d'emploi* in the hope that his understanding of French might help him glean enough information to begin his search.

One in particular draws his attention: *L'agent de sécurité*, it reads. The vacancy is for a security guard at one of the more prestigious Montmartre gallery museums, and if Chester's translation is correct, it is a nighttime job. His heart races. The work would suit him well as it would demand very little interaction and give him time to write. He pictures himself dressed in uniform, parading the halls of the gallery, alone. In between checks, he would write at his desk. He pulls out his guidebook and locates the gallery, which is situated on the second tier of the *butte* and currently open to visitors. He assesses his current state of dress and decides he is fit enough to at least make enquiries. Armed with the newspaper, he descends the hill, hoping the position has not already been filled.

A formal interview the following day secures the job for Chester, albeit on a trial basis. He cannot believe his luck. It seems that night shift work in one's own company failed to attract many applicants. The salary is enough to cover his rent and basic living costs, so he is more than happy. What pleases him most is that he has been allocated a small office space, one used by other staff during the daytime, from which to manage his duties which mainly consist of ensuring the building is securely locked and that no prowlers or would-be thieves lurk in dark corners. The rest of the time he will be free to sit at the desk and write.

Two out of the three tenants with whom he shares the apartment block work during the day, which means he is able to sleep peacefully for a few hours when he returns from his shift. The third tenant, an elderly lady with swollen ankles and a black cat, is rarely heard, except when she is cooking, and even then he is more aware of the smell than the noise. She really does love garlic.

It takes Chester approximately three weeks to begin to adapt to the nocturnal way of life. The work at the gallery is unchallenging and mundane, but the opportunity to write more than makes up for it. He spends at least two or three hours every night in the head of his alter ego, Runo Quill, and is getting to know him quite well. Sometimes he dreams of selling his work but fails to convince himself of his potential as a professional writer.

In the weeks following his arrival at Montmartre he has plucked up the courage to ask after the clown by the name of Geppetto at the Théâtre Déjazet, albeit half-heartedly, pre-surmising that his questions would be met with a negative response. However, not once has he felt inclined to see Pierrot perform again. The memory brings him out in goosebumps. It seemed as though Pierrot had reached inside his soul and stolen it to use as a mime puppet.

Each and every morning, when he arrives home from his shift, he scans the mail propped in the hallway in case Eveline has replied to his postcard. His patience is rewarded at the end of the third week when he spies his name on an envelope. Ensconced in his room, he tears it open, surprised to see a second envelope folded inside. He puts it to one side and skims the letter. She writes that she is pleased he is settled and hopes he has found work. He remembers then how in his haste to inform her of his address he had done so as soon as he had signed the tenancy agreement instead of waiting until he found a job. What will she think of his lowly profession?

He continues to the bottom of the page, then flips it to the other side. What he reads next knocks him sideways.

With regards to the story of Arlecchino, I cannot express how much I enjoyed it. You undoubtedly have a talent for writing, Chester, which brings me to my next point. (Picture me taking a deep breath.) I hope you won't get mad at me, but I have sold your story to an arts magazine here in Florence, hence the second envelope containing payment of fifty francs. It will be published under your name, of course, and they have asked you to send more if you are willing. Chester, it was simply too good to sit idle on my desk, so I translated it into Italian with a little help from Arnaldo and sent it off.

If I have done wrong, then so be it, and if I never hear from you again I will understand. However, I hope that's not the case. Please consider carefully before making any hasty decisions.

Yours,

Eveline

Chester slumps back in the chair. This is more than he could have hoped. All the time he'd been imagining Eveline's response to his work, but not once did he picture this. The letter trembles in his outstretched hand, as though afraid it has upset him. The words Eveline has written swim in his vision, losing clarity, so that he believes he imagined them. He reads it a second time before opening the second envelope. In his hand he holds a brand new fifty franc note, enough to cover the rent for a week, and all because of one story. Though part of him is a little mad at her audacity, he is absurdly pleased. *They want more*, he thinks, in disbelief. He must reply to her right away or else she might think him ungrateful.

High on adrenaline, Chester is too wound up to sleep, so he washes and changes into clean clothes before heading into town. Cobbled pavement and labyrinthine alleyways do their best to add to his sense of confusion. Montmartre is a Minotaur's maze. Narrow streets that twist and turn, and flights of steps that leave him breathless. It seems to Chester that every time he ventures into the streets he discovers something new.

He slips his hand inside his pocket and smooths the surface of the fifty franc note. Frugal at heart but wilted from his night shift and lack of breakfast, he sits at a pavement cafe, not far from the Moulin Rouge, and drinks in the sights, treating himself to a couple of sweet pastries and a pot of coffee in the hope that they might revive him. Portrait artists tout for trade on street corners, shadow puppeteers vie for the crowd's attention wherever there's space. Stalls and kiosks; men playing boules.

Within a few minutes of draining his coffee, a waiter appears with the bill concealed inside a leather folder with the name of the cafe emblazoned on the front, then hurries indoors. Chester opens the folder and gasps. His bill is inside, but there is something else, too—a playing card—the Queen of Hearts. He glances behind him, towards the door of the cafe, just in time to see a gentleman dressed head to toe in black. The magician! Chester is certain. He pays Chester a perfunctory nod before marching down the street at a steady pace.

Chester gets to his feet, eager to follow him. In one hand he holds the Queen of Hearts; in the other, the bill. He must pay first. He hurries inside the cafe and approaches the counter. "The gentleman," he says, "dressed in black."

The waiter, who is polishing the glassware, frowns.

"He was here a moment ago. I saw him leave."

A shake of the head.

"Oh, never mind," Chester says, eager to take his leave. He hands the waiter the bill and a five franc note, leaving behind a far too generous tip, then hurries into the street.

At the far end is the magician. His pace has not slowed, so Chester must run if he is to catch up with him. Breathless and perspiring, he weaves in and out of passers-by, but all too soon the magician disappears around the corner and is lost.

Chester gives chase, up a flight of steps and along the next street, but no matter how much he hurries the magician outpaces him. Not once does the man in black turn around, he simply continues to wend his way from one street to the next, climbing each flight of steps within the *butte* with the ease of an athlete.

The higher he climbs, the narrower the streets become, until they are no more than shadowed alleys. This is a part of town Chester has not yet explored. It has a timeless quality, less garish, with Medieval buildings that threaten to topple and dogs that howl like the devil. Tall chimneys billow woodsmoke and the distant sound of a clarinet gives the place a dream-like aura.

He is tempted to call out, but what would he say?

The higher he climbs, the more unsure of himself he grows. At the foot of another flight of steps he pauses, hands on knees, gulping air. Fit and lean though he is, he cannot match the flight of the man dressed in black. The Queen of Hearts grows warm in the palm of his hand. He pockets the card and continues down the street.

In the distance the magician stops momentarily, before disappearing inside one of the buildings at the far end of the street.

Chester hurries onward, then stops outside the building that he is certain the magician entered, a building no bigger than any one of the quaint houses.

Le Petit Théâtre des Particularités—The Little Theatre of Peculiarities, a sign above the door reads.

Chester peers in at the window. The theatre is in darkness. He tries the door handle but finds it well and truly locked. No sign of the man in black anywhere. Arms outstretched, he leans against the wooden door frame, catching his breath. No bell to ring, no knocker to rap at, but a poster pinned to the door reads: *Samedi Soir, Le Fantôme de Colette Claudel*—Saturday Night, The Ghost of Colette Claudel. The poster is monochrome, the words revealed through a sketch of the open curtains of the theatre stage. Skulls and masks adorn the border, but it does not say who the play is written by, nor does it name the actors. Come to think of it, it doesn't even state the time of the performance. How frustrating. He will need to make further enquiries, as since his weekends are free, he would love to attend.

He idles for a while, hoping the magician will reappear. The window to the left displays a series of photographs of actors donned in masks. In one, a young woman dressed in white tulle and the half-mask of a phoenix is seated on a threadbare armchair, her expression gloomy. Beside her stands a child, a young girl around the age of six. The child rests one hand on the woman's knee but does not look at her. A black dragon mask covers most of the child's face, in contrast to her simple pinafore and bare feet.

Chester spends long enough in front of the theatre window to notice how silent the street is, how sleepy. Fatigue hits, so he turns on his heels, defeated. He has not taken more than two or three paces when an elderly gentleman, dressed in labourer's clothes, comes limping down the street. He pauses in his step when he sees Chester.

"*Excusez-moi, monsieur*," Chester says, returning to the theatre door. He points at the poster. "*Quelle heure?*"

The man screws up his face. "*Huh! Minuit. Toujours minuit.*" He shakes his head in disapproval before continuing his journey.

Midnight, always midnight. What a strange time to perform a play. Chester counts the days until Saturday, relishing the thought of returning to this strange little theatre. Something tells him the performances here are not the usual kind.

11

Dear Eveline,

I'm still reeling from the shock of your letter. The fact that you sold the story of Arlecchino to a magazine is...well, it's ridiculous, inexcusable, but also incredibly exciting. I forgave you within seconds and believe you have given me the impetus I need to try my hand at a professional writing career. So yes, of course I will send another story. In fact, I have included it with this letter. The story is called The Three Lives of Quasimodo, and since the original was penned by the great Victor Hugo in Florence, I am hopeful they might consider it relevant.

So much has happened since I sent you the postcard. I am working as a nighttime security guard at the Musée d'art Moderne here in Montmartre, which affords me ample time to write. Needless to say, I have not yet found Geppetto. In fact, he is proving rather elusive, though I believe wholeheartedly that I will meet him soon. His suggestion that I study the performance of Pierrot almost proved to be my undoing, but I shall tell you more about that when we meet, which I hope will be soon. Which brings me to my next point...

Eveline, you would love it here in Montmartre. In this part of the city, the arts are thriving. The streets are littered with galleries and theatres of all kinds. Please consider paying me a visit. I would dearly love you to be my guest, and of course I would arrange suitable accommodation on your behalf.

At this time of year, the streets are rousing from slumber and are donned in colourful coats and twinkling lights that sparkle almost as brightly as you do.

Give my kind regards to Arnaldo and thank him for help-ing you to translate the story.

Write soon, and let me know if you intend to visit.

I miss you already,

Chester

Chester adds The Three Lives of Quasimodo to the letter, then seals the envelope before his nerves get the better of him. I miss you already. What was he thinking? He sticks the stamp onto the envelope and walks to the nearest mailbox. A moment's hesitation before the envelope is swallowed by the dark void, seizing ownership of the document.

Since seeing the man who he believes to be the magician disappear inside the strange little theatre, Chester has been eager to revisit, though not entirely certain if he will be able to find the place again. The warren of streets that make up Montmartre have no obvious layout other than the fact that they become steeper and steeper the higher one climbs.

As for the playing card of the Queen of Hearts, he now uses it as a place-marker for Geppetto's journal and cannot help but wonder if he and the magician are somehow connected. His imagination concocts all kinds of scenarios. Was the magician known to Geppetto? Is it possible he was asked to place the journal in a location where Chester would find it? But if so, the magician would have had to spend every day at the Reading Rooms waiting for Chester to come along, which makes no sense at all. He has even considered the possibility that the magician and Geppetto are one and the same, which means he is here, in Montmartre, watching Chester's every move.

By the time Saturday comes around he cannot wait to see what *Le Petit Théâtre des Particularités* will offer. Perhaps the magician, having led him there (for Chester truly believes this to be the case), will finally show his hand.

After a few hours of sleep to recover from his night shift, Chester walks the streets in an attempt to relocate the theatre. It had taken some considerable time to find his way home after his first visit, and he had made several wrong turns, but today he follows his instinct and locates it within twenty minutes of leaving home. It is as it was previous—in darkness and locked. Nothing has changed over the last few days: same posters, same photographs in the window. The only notable difference is that today a pack of playing cards lie splayed in a fan formation inside the window. Chester scans their contents, amused to discover the Queen of Hearts is missing. He pictures the missing card secreted inside Geppetto's journal, marking the last page of his previous entry, the one that instructed Chester to follow him to Paris.

If he doesn't show up here, where will Geppetto send him next? His stomach somersaults at the thought of moving again. He is beginning to settle in Montmartre, starting to discover the real Chester. He pictures Eveline here with him. Could they make a life together? And if so, would he abandon his mission to find the former clown? The idea of doing so seems sacrilegious, as if he would be letting the man down. He shrugs the idea away and heads for home, but tonight, before midnight, he will return.

Apart from a few stars that shine like silver buttons, the sky wears a black shroud. A nip in the air forces Chester's hands deep inside his pockets. Or is it excitement that makes him shiver? In typical Chester fashion, he arrives outside *Le Petit Théâtre des Particularités* with thirty minutes to spare, and yet he is not the first to arrive. Two couples and a lone gentleman are here before him. Though eager to ask if tickets to see *Le Fantôme de Colette Claudel* will be available at the door, he lacks the confidence to strike up a conversation. Over the last few weeks his understanding of French has improved somewhat, but he is still a long way from making conversation. Instead, he listens...and watches.

Others join the queue until the line snakes its way along the street and almost to the corner. His breath is a ghost that wisps its way towards the lips of strangers in the hope of gleaning information. Moments later, the sign above the door of the theatre blinks to life and lights appear in the window. Chester takes a deep breath as those ahead of him move forward.

No kiosk on entering, instead welcoming them inside is a sylphlike woman, dressed as a spectre. Hollow-eyed, chiselled cheekbones, her face painted the colour of ash. Her slender wrist is draped in silver bracelets that tinkle as she passes a printed leaflet to each spectator. She does so without smiling, and in return they hand her two francs, which she slips inside a gauze bag, draped on her shoulder. Chester follows suit, then heads through the foyer and into the auditorium.

A lone pianist, dressed in white, plays a sombre tune, subduing the conversation of those who enter. The stage wears heavy maroon drapes, and the ceiling is painted like an astral plane.

Row by row, the theatre fills until not a single seat remains. The lights dim, and the show begins.

Some ninety minutes later, Chester rises from his seat, shaken by what he has seen. A ghost story, yes, but *Le Fantôme de Colette Claudel* has been more than that, much more. No clanking chains or jump scares, but something quite unique. He does not know how the theatre company managed the tangible changes in temperature and the sensation of having one's hair raked by invisible fingers, nor does he wish to know. He would prefer to believe it is magical. No wonder the theatre calls itself *peculiar.*

A thought occurs as he is leaving, one buoyed by his most recent work, though it makes him feel nauseous, too. On the way out, he will question the possibility of providing material for future performances. He idles close to the auditorium exit in the pretence of waiting for someone, until just a few stragglers remain.

The foyer is a chapel of rest, dimly lit with candles and oil lamps that scent the air. The spectre who ushered them in stands close to the door, bidding the last few people a *bonne nuit.*

Chester takes a deep breath and musters up the courage to speak to her. "An excellent performance," he says. "*Merci.*"

"We aim to please," she says, her voice a whisper. The shadows beneath her eyes give her the appearance of someone who has one foot in the grave.

"I wonder," he says. "Who writes your material?"

Her blue lips twitch, and her eyes twinkle beneath the lights. "We have several writers, but they all have something special. Something...how you say?" She places a finger beneath her chin and tilts her head towards the ceiling. "In France, we call it *je ne sais quoi*. It is a quality that cannot easily be described." A slight shrug. "We know it when we see it."

"I see. A-and if, for example, I wanted to offer some material for you to consider, how would I go about it?"

She studies his face, taking her time, and Chester's bowels constrict.

"You see, I've always worked in theatre. I-I used to be a clown. A tragic clown. B-but now, I write." He cannot believe those words have escaped his lips. Part of him wants to make a quick exit, but a more daring part whispers *the worst is over, wait and see.*

The bracelets on her arm jingle as she reaches for a card on the desk, and Chester sees that the bracelets are filled with charms, everything from a skull to a butterfly.

"Send it in," she says, handing Chester the card. "If we like it, we'll get in touch. But remember, it will need to be a very peculiar kind of writing."

The journey home feels like walking on air. Chester's feet refuse to touch the ground, and his head is in the clouds. *Why not*, he thinks, *you have nothing to lose.*

And the imagined face of Geppetto, and that of the magician in black, wink their approval.

12

Chester has scripted The Raven and the Tightrope Walker and The City of Silence and is working on a third script when the letter from Eveline arrives. She is thrilled to hear he has settled, and even more pleased that he has forgiven her for selling his story. She also writes that the same magazine wishes to purchase The Three Lives of Quasimodo, which raises his hope for the trilogy he is working on. He will be forever indebted to Eveline, regardless of how their relationship plays out.

She agrees to visit at the end of May and asks that he arrange a hotel room on her behalf. The visit will take place over the weekend, when Chester is not at work. He puts down the letter and gazes around his humble abode. Perhaps he can paint the walls before she visits, buy a few soft furnishings to brighten the place.

Right now, his nerves are too frazzled to continue writing, so instead he takes a clean sheet of paper and compiles a list of the places he would like Eveline to see. He will have but a weekend to make her fall in love with Montmartre...and him.

Three things happen on the morning Eveline is due to arrive. He is awoken at the break of dawn by a dream, a dream in which the man in black challenges him to a game of poker with the loser forfeiting his right hand to a silver sword. Is the dream an omen? Chester has never played poker, so he is certain to lose. Since Eveline is due to arrive today, he cannot help but associate the dream with her proposed visit. She has become his right hand. Without her, the progress he has made will collapse. Is this what the magician is trying to tell him?

But he is not worthy of Eveline. She is too beautiful and far too clever for the likes of him. This he is sure she will realize within minutes of them meeting again. Who does he think he is? He's just a clown disguised as a writer.

How to calm himself? Before he has a chance to do so, a rattle in the hallway announces the arrival of mail. It could be for any one of the tenants, but he cannot rid himself of the notion that it is a letter from Eveline, explaining that she has changed her mind and won't be coming to Paris after all. Despite being dressed in his underwear, he runs downstairs to the hallway and picks up the post with a trembling hand. The letter is indeed addressed to him. He hurries upstairs and tears it open.

The letter is from *Le Petit Théâtre des Particularités* stating that they very much enjoyed his scripted trilogy and would like to arrange a meeting to discuss the prospect of purchasing it for performance. Chester is elated, and yet he has not fully recovered from the sense of foreboding the dream left him with. *It won't work out*, he tells himself. *This life of which you dream is not for the likes of you.*

The third significant event of the morning is that having scrutinized the contents of the letter from the theatre repeatedly, he sees that Geppetto's journal is sitting on his desk, not in the bedside drawer where he keeps it stowed. The Queen of Hearts protrudes from a page further along in the book, and his breath stalls.

Flipping the journal to the playing card marker he reads:

So here we are in Montmartre, Paris.

Having lured you here to witness Pierrot's performance, I have to admit to being a little disappointed by your response. It seems you were not as impressed by him as I was, but that is okay, we all have our preferences, I guess.

This is not the case at all. It is not that Chester wasn't impressed by Pierrot. In some ways quite the opposite. He saw too much of himself reflected in Pierrot, that is all.

But how has Geppetto managed to glean his reaction to Pierrot's performance without them having spoken? The sense of being watched rears its head again.

Geppetto talks about his time in Paris, Montmartre in particular. It seems that like Chester he too was impressed by the prolific number of galleries and theatres in this part of the city and the way in which the arts thrive here.

The final paragraph of the journal entry comes as a shock:

I imagine you'll be eager to hear where I want you to go next. Are you ready? The next leg of our journey will require you to cross the ocean all the way to the United States of America. Trust me, Chester, the art of clowning is thriving there.

They have circus acts that travel by train, would you believe? Why, they even take large mammals along with them, such as elephants and tigers!

Chester slams the journal shut and tosses it onto the bed. What is Geppetto playing at? Here he is, beginning to make a new life for himself in Montmartre. He does not wish to travel across the ocean, nor does he wish to join a circus that roams the country, especially if it takes wild animals with it. The concept is cruel.

Has Geppetto played him for a fool all this time? Is he and the magician laughing at Chester's expense?

He picks up the letter from *Le Petit Théâtre des Particularités* and reads it again. This is what he wants—to write! He never wants to see or hear a clown again as long as he lives. *Well in that case, you'd better not look in the mirror*, a voice inside him says.

After a meagre breakfast, Chester turns his attention to Eveline's visit. A range of emotion swells in his heart when he thinks of her. She is like a sickness that he cannot overcome.

He studies his reflection in the mirror, his profile, his pallor, then wiggles his toes in his shoes. If he is not mistaken, his feet have shrunk. Either that, or his shoes have stretched with wear. Perhaps it is time he bought a new pair, from a proper shoe shop. But surely that would not be possible. They would never fit.

Chester waits at the station with his heart in his mouth. When Eveline's train pulls in, he hardly dares to look. She alights, wearing a wide smile and an ever wider-brimmed hat.

She looks glorious, and for the umpteenth time that day, Chester reminds himself that she has come because of him.

An exchange of air kisses, he takes her luggage, and she takes his spare hand without hesitating. "It's so good to see you, Chester," she says. "You look well. Less gaunt than when I saw you last."

He laughs. "I guess that's a compliment, so I'll accept it graciously. It's good to see you too, Eveline." He pauses in his stride and sighs. "In fact, you have no idea just how good it is."

"I have something for you," she says, pointing to the suitcase. "In there."

Chester has not bought her a gift. In fact, it did not cross his mind to do so. "I hope you haven't spent your hard-earned money on me. I-I— "

"No," she says. "It cost me nothing but time, but I'm nervous in case you won't like it."

It must be a portrait, Chester thinks. "Of course I will," he says, squeezing her hand. Inside though, he dreads opening the gift. It's enough that he has to look at himself in the mirror, never mind look at a portrait. "I imagine you're hungry," he says, changing the subject. "I know I am."

They lunch at a small patio cafe, and Chester cannot remember when last he felt this happy, this content. The conversation flows, and he relaxes into Eveline's company. To him, she shines. Vivacious, an open book that he wishes to devour from cover to cover.

"Would you like to check in at the hotel first?" he asks when she suggests seeing his place.

"Whatever you think best," she says.

"My apartment, Eveline. It's—well it's not up to much, I must warn you. But if the writing takes off, perhaps I—"

She places a finger across his lips to silence him. "Hush. I do not care what your apartment looks like. All I care about is your happiness. I would like to return to Florence with an image of you nestled in your home, nothing more."

Chester waits in the hotel lobby while Eveline unpacks. Within minutes she appears, carrying a purse and a parcel wrapped in brown paper. It is evident from the shape of the parcel that it is indeed a painting. "The gift," she says, "I don't want you to open it until we reach your home, though." She shrugs and looks downhearted. "That way, if you don't like it—"

He feigns a smile. "Let me guess. You've painted my portrait?" He releases a slow breath which hangs in the air, suspended.

"You'll see," she says, her face flushed.

Chester's apartment is cool and airy. The sharp tang of lavender wafts through the open window, welcoming Eveline with a floral bouquet. She casts her gaze around the room which Chester has freshly painted in a pale-blue hue. "It's fabulous," she says. "It suits you well. Neat and—" Finger to bottom lip, she searches for the word. "Succinct." She flings herself onto the bed and grins.

"Succinct?"

"Chester, you do not waste words, not during conversation I mean. Now, when it comes to your writing it's a different matter altogether." She puts a hand to her mouth. "I don't mean to suggest that you waste words when you write. What I mean is that your writing is far more..." She twirls a wrist in the air. "Adventurous." She holds both his hands and gazes up at him. "But in real life you are far too shy, too modest, and that is something that needs to change."

The gift remains unopened on the table, where Chester had placed it on arrival. "Go on," she says. "Open it."

He picks it up and begins to unwrap, while she sits at the edge of the bed, biting her fist.

Chester is equally nervous. A lifetime of wearing his emotions on his face has made him incapable of hiding them. The final sheet of wrapping paper tumbles to the floor, revealing the portrait.

Chester holds it in front of him, arms outstretched and shoulders tense. But within moments his whole body relaxes. "You know," he says, "I was afraid you'd painted me and that I wouldn't know how to react." He studies the painting of a man, around the same age as he is. The man is seated at a desk, immersed in the act of writing. Except he isn't. A notebook lies open on the desk, and it's true that he holds a pen, but he is not writing. His eyes are closed, the fingers of his left hand placed just so on his forehead as though he is trying to think of a word that is hidden from view.

"Chester?" Eveline's voice is timid, her tone uncertain.

He glances from painting to Eveline. "I love it. Thank you so much." He focuses again on the painting. "This will always remind me of you, and the way in which you helped me to find myself." His voice strains.

"Chester, what do you mean you were afraid I had painted you?" She frowns and reddens. She gets to her feet and joins him, leaning against his shoulder. "Do you not see the likeness? I made it more true to life than I usually do. Unlike the painting of Arnaldo, I wanted you to be able to see yourself as you really are."

His face falls. "But—" His eyes roam over the portrait, drinking in the detail. Granted, both he and the subject are of similar age. They even wear the same clothes, but there the likeness ends. "The nose," he says, shaking his head. "It's not mine." He covers his own with his hand, embarrassed by the overly large feature. The subject's nose is of average size. In fact, he'd go as far as to say it's a handsome nose.

Eveline takes the portrait from him and lays it down on the table. She holds his chin and gazes into his eyes, her expression weary. "Of course it's your nose," she says. "And your hair, your chin, your hands. Do you not see?"

He looks again. The hair, perhaps...and the chin. He studies his hand. Long fingers, bony knuckles. Granted, it is similar to the man's in the painting. But the nose? "Eveline, I think you are just trying to be kind, and I appreciate your kindness, but this is not me. It will never be me." He takes a step backwards.

Her eyes fill with tears. "Do you have a mirror?"

He frowns. "Of course. How else would I shave?"

"Then show me."

He hesitates, but he knows better than to deny her. He leads the way down the hall and into the tiny bathroom, stopping in front of the mirror.

"Go on," she says. "I want you to see what others see."

When they return to the sitting room, Chester is overcome. The incident with the mirror has left him reeling.

"Take off your shoes," she says.

"My shoes?" He cannot bear to do so.

"Yes, your shoes." She pushes him onto the bed, then lifts his right foot.

"Stop!"

"Then do it yourself."

He looks at her and sees defiance staring back. She chews her lower lip. No hint of a smile, the woman for whom laughter is never far away is deadly serious.

He hesitates, but gives in and removes one shoe.

Eveline picks it up and places it beside his foot. "You see." A desperate sigh. "The shoe is inches longer than your foot, Chester. Look at it, for pity's sake!"

He stares at his feet, as though seeing them for the first time. She is right. But how? Can feet shrink?

Head in hands, he rocks to and fro.

Eveline sits beside him, her expression gentler now. "Chester, if you want to be happy you must accept yourself for who you really are. No one can do that for you."

Eventually, he speaks. "But how do I put the past behind me while I still bear the scars?"

She strokes the back of his hand. "The scars are internal, not physical, and therefore only you can heal them."

Time stands still, even the air in the room holds its breath.

"Listen," she says. "You're happy here, and you're on the brink of achieving the kind of life you always dreamed about. You mustn't let anything stop you, Chester."

He sniffs. "I am happy here. Happier than I have been for a very long time. But there's another problem."

She meets his gazes and waits.

"The journal," he says. "Geppetto wants me to follow his footsteps across the Atlantic to America."

She swallows. "Can I see it?"

"See what? The journal?"

"Yes, Chester. The journal."

He gets to his feet and removes it from the drawer, hobbling from the lack of a shoe.

"Just this morning," he says. "He must have written it while I was at work, though how he got in I do not know."

She narrows her gaze, takes the journal from him, and wanders over to the table.

The air breathes again, warm and lavender scented. Chester puts his shoe back on, while Eveline scrutinizes the book for some considerable time.

"And your notebook," she says. "The one you're writing your latest story in."

"What of it?"

"Can I see that, too?"

Chester hesitates. "It's only a draft, a work in progress. I don't really—"

She holds out a hand, as if his refusal is not an option. He hands her the notebook and paces the room while she reads.

Several minutes later she says, "Sit, Chester. We need to talk." She places the journal and notebook so that they are side by side on the table.

He pulls up a chair and waits, his breath short and sharp.

She points at both books, her expression solemn. "Chester, can you not see?"

He follows her finger as she points at both books in turn.

"The curve of the *s*, the loop of the *y*... The writing is yours."

"The notebook, you mean?" He fidgets in his chair, exasperated.

"*And* the journal."

He shakes his head. "The writing is similar, I grant you, but the journal belongs to Geppetto. I found it in the Reading Rooms, in Magician's Quarter."

A dull ache spreads from behind his eyes to the top of his head, and all the way down his neck. His breathing is laboured, his hands clenched into fists. What is she suggesting?

When he eventually looks at her, he sees that her eyes are brimming with tears.

"Geppetto," she says, "is, I suggest, your alter ego. A man you invented so that you could escape the life that held you bound."

He pushes back his chair and stands. "Impossible. I've seen him, or at least I've seen the magician, the man I believe is working for Geppetto. You might think me mad, but I've seen him with my own eyes!"

"And what evidence do you have, other than your imagination?" Her words are not unkind, simply probing.

He snorts, exasperated. "The playing card. The Queen of Hearts." He snatches the journal from the table and shakes it, expecting the Queen of Hearts to tumble to the floor. But it does not. He flips through the pages, but the Queen of Hearts is missing. "It must have fallen out," he says, pulling out the drawer and rummaging about.

But the Queen of Hearts is nowhere to be seen, at least not in the form of a playing card.

Instead, she sits at his table, waiting for the man she has grown most fond of to gather his wits and realize that he can no longer run away from himself.

Epilogue

C hester and Eveline sit centre stage in the front row of *Le Petit Théâtre des Particularités*, her hand clenched tightly in his. Six whole months have passed since his first visit, longer still since he last saw London.

His free hand surreptitiously strokes the outline of his nose, liking what it finds there. He glances down at his feet, but it's far too dark to see. And in any case, what does it matter? Father Roly's clown skeleton, The Clown God Cholly, the mysterious magician. None of it matters, because tonight, at the witching hour, Chester will witness for the first time his words performed on stage. He shakes his head to erase the memories, gazes in awe as tiny particles of sparkling silver swirl in front of his face before drifting down the aisle, then turns his attention to the stage.

The curtains open, and the backdrop heralds the debut of the trilogy.

Death of a Clown; Birth of an Artist,
by Runo Quill
A life of redemption in three acts

Zar walks the tightrope with ease, head held high and feet perfectly balanced. A raven perches on Zar's shoulder, its wings outspread in perfect symmetry with Zar's arms. Every now and then, the stage lights catch the iridescent wings of the raven, turning them into lightning streaks of indigo and gold, a warning of the storm yet to come.

As the blade of the knife strikes, and Zar tumbles into the river, the audience holds its collective breath, and when the ghost of Zar claims his first victim a few fail to suppress a cheer.

Act Two, and the Emperor sits on a golden throne, issuing a decree that from this day forth, no one in the town will be permitted to ask questions. Much of the act is performed through mime, the theme such that it calls for much gesture and facial expression. Eveline steals glimpses at the audience who have fallen under the Emperor's spell, for they, too, are silent.

A short intermission before the third and final act, an intermission during which Chester remains in his seat, too nervous to mingle in case he should hear disparaging thoughts expressed. But that is not the case, for Eveline does so on his behalf, and returns to report that the audience is delighted.

The third and final act, titled *Death of a Clown; Birth of an Artist*, opens with high jinks as a white-faced clown with a glum expression performs tricks on stage among his troupe. A mock crime scene, one in which the perpetrators, who are all clowns, make so many errors that they give the game away. As the clown police arrive on the scene, the melancholic clown climbs a rope ladder in an attempt to escape, while his partners in crime flee on foot.

An error of judgement makes his foot catch in the rope, and the tragic clown is left dangling mid-air as the ladder swings just out of reach of the clown police.

The scene Chester has written is the scene that acted as the catalyst for his escape from the life he once knew. His heart pounds in his chest as he remembers the sense of detachment he had felt as he had swung from the ladder above the audience. How their grinning faces had appeared monstrous to him, and how he had wanted so desperately to escape.

Sensing his mood, Eveline squeezes his hand, and in doing so brings him back to the present.

As coloured spotlights sweep across the faces of the audience, the music changes from jovial to bleak.

Only Chester knows what is about to happen. He has not even told Eveline.

The clown's life is about to end.

The audience screams as the clown leaps from ladder to stage, arms and legs flailing. A sickening thud as his body hits the ground. The stage turns black.

At this moment in time, it would be possible to hear a pin drop.

An adagio in D minor, each note of the violin the tug of a heartstring. The stage is resurrected by flickering candles that dance in the breeze. Centre stage stands a book, as tall as a man, a book bound in ox-blood leather, the words *Death of a Clown; Birth of an Artist* inscribed on the front.

The sound of the violin is replaced by a solo clarinet, the tune haunting, like notes from the satyr, Pan's, flute.

A gust of wind; the pages flutter. Then, from behind the book, out crawls a man. Slowly, one limb at a time, he stands and faces the audience. Naked except for a loincloth, his skin slick with amniotic fluid and hair plastered to his scalp. His hands and face are smeared with streaks of greasepaint, so that it is evident that this man and the white-faced clown are one and the same. Noble features, tall and slender, with a ribcage reminiscent of Jesus's on the cross.

The book rotates on its axis, until blank pages face the audience. Violin and clarinet play in harmony and are joined by the ethereal sound of the flute, summoning to mind the heart of the woods and the mythical springs of Arcadia.

A pen is propped against the book's gutter. The metamorphosed man picks it up, and with his back to the audience, he signs his name: *Runo Quill*.

Black ink on a white face, the name indelible.

He bows, then walks off stage, light-footed, as though walking on air.

Chester Brown, the former clown, turns to his queen, all dressed in red, and smiles.

Quick Favor

Thank you so much for dedicating your time to reading this book! May we ask a quick favor?

Will you please take a moment to leave a review on Amazon, Goodreads, or wherever you purchased the book? Your words have power. Your review can help this book reach more readers. We appreciate you!

Acknowledgments

As writers we spend the majority of our time alone, bashing away at the keys until something acceptable takes shape before our eyes. The journey can seem a lonely one, and yet there are many who help us along the way.

First of all I would like to thank my husband, Tony, without whose encouragement and wisdom this book would not exist. You are my first reader, my harshest critic, my best friend, the brains behind the cover, and most of all...my life.

Immense thanks and appreciation to my publishers, Lucas Marino and Les Hernandez of Sobelo Books, for believing in this story. Your professionalism, hard work, and enthusiasm along the way has meant so much.

Last but not least, to each and every reader, without whom my work would have no purpose.

Sincere appreciation always,
Catherine McCarthy

About The Author

Catherine McCarthy weaves dark tales on an ancient loom from her farmhouse in West Wales. Her previous works include the collection *Mists and Megaliths* and numerous novels and novellas including *Immortelle*, *A Moonlit Path of Madness*, *Mosaic*, *The Wolf and the Favour*, and *The House at the End of Lacelean Street*. Her short fiction has been published in various anthologies and magazines, including those by House of Gamut, Black Spot Books, and Dark Matter Ink.

In 2020 she won the Aberystwyth University Prize for her short fiction.

Time away from the loom is spent hiking the Welsh coast path or huddled in an ancient graveyard reading Dylan Thomas or Poe.

www.ingramcontent.com/pod-product-compliance
Lightning Source LLC
Chambersburg PA
CBHW031051310726
48969CB00007B/2215